The Boy

Thank You

There are a lot of people out there that don't believe in me or my ideas. Though many people have come to me for advice and they either listen or don't. So, to the people who don't listen and don't support me in my art and times of need, I wish you a good day and a good life. Thank You for leaving me alone.

There is a group of people that have supported me and made me excited to work on this and continued to push me to finish this project. Thank you to all of you that supported me on Facebook and all the like buttons pushed and the comments that were placed. Some funny or general questions, either way it helped me at times when I was down.

During my darkest days, I found myself without a purpose, without a reason to move forward. These times were the toughest of my life and I want to thank those who grabbed me and pulled me up from the fetal position and allowed me to cry away the sorrow that lived inside on their shoulder. To those people I owe you my life. They go from doctors to the people that I will always call my family and I will stand beside now for the rest of my days. Those people are very few as they stood beside me while others shunned me. They were the ones that gave me strength at home and at work which gave me life once again. Without them I would not have reached deep into my sick and twisted mind to create what will become my personal master pieces. Thank You Brad, Autumn, Clay, Jocelyn, Brandon, Kris, Laura, Jeremy, Becca, and the few others that remain nameless. Without you all, I would not be who I am today. To my family, Thank You for leaving me with myself and not trying to change me. I am who I am. If I have forgotten anyone I am sorry but this is when you look back at the process and you see who was there for you. To the named you supported me not just in the writing but in life. Thank you again.

Introduction Too My World

I have sat back and have watched the world pass me by. While it moved I watched people and how they interacted with others around them. In my long studies of humans, I have learned that we are made to do and believe in a greater power of people. They believe that there is a greater good to be fulfilled or that we must be controlled so the masses don't take over their perfect existence. They have changed the moral fabric of human nature to fit their needs. The Bible has been changed so many times its hilarious. What if coming up in the ages that the names of Satan and God had been switched? Most people now would be praising the all mighty Satan and he would have a son named Jesus or some other very popular name for the time.

My point is that reality is what we make it. Everything around us can be changed to whatever we want. There should be no holding anyone back from

4

anything they want to do. Everyone knows their moral compass but religion shouldn't dictate it or add to it. We know it inside our selves but we don't listen to it. We listen to what the mass media tells you to believe. Disconnect yourself and listen to what is inside of you. You can call it God or Jesus or even Satan or whatever religion you may be but it's not. Its evolution inside of you pointing you towards tomorrow so you can evolve. Unplug from the mass media, it will only rot your brain and give you anxiety. Come to peace within yourself.

Chapter 1

"Come here boy. Hold the pigs head still."

The boy tries to hold the pig the best he can.

"No, your dumbass, like this!" He reached around and slit the pig's throat and laughed as the pig tried to run and squeal. The boy turned his head so he wouldn't have to watch. He didn't want to see death again.

"You better be watching boy. You need to get used of this shit if you're ever going to run this farm. You'll probably let it fall to pieces." The father reached down and grabbed his son under the chin and above his head and held him facing the dying animal.

"I said you better be fucking watching you little shit!" The boy watched out of fear of what his father might do to him. Then his eyes started tearing with a drop falling from his eye and ran down on his father's hand.

"Little pussy, go and get the knives so we can cut your little friend up." The father spoke in a sarcastic voice to annoy the son even more.

The boy did as he was told to appease him. He stood over his father and watched as he pulled out the insides all over the ground. The boy just stood there with tears in his eyes, knowing that he would have to eat his friend soon.

The boy grew up on a farm and helped his father take care of it. Killing animals to eat was normal, but this one was special to the boy. The boy had become friends with the pig. There were no other children around this farm. There wasn't even anyone around for miles. It was just the boy and his father. They were so far back into nowhere that people probably didn't even know they were there. Only occasionally the father would go to town to buy or sell things for the farm.

The day before the boy was outside playing with the pig in secret. The father never knew of the friendship. He never allowed the boy anything extra, no fun just work. The boy didn't have toys and if he made one then the father would burn it. The life he was being set up for was a lonely one and that did not go over well with the boy. So, he made a friend that couldn't be burned, but forgot that he could be killed.

Later, the father sat and drank moonshine late into the hours of the night. He didn't know what to do with the boy. He couldn't have his son having a pig as a friend. The boy should just be lucky that he was alive, let alone a roof over his head. All that matters are that and nothing else. Everything else is wasteful and should not be had.

Early in the morning is when the father made up his mind that the pig had to die. He woke the boy up and took him out and said that the pig was to die. The boy wanted to argue, but he knew it would be worse on the pig if he did. Dying was bad enough but he didn't want his father to make him suffer even more.

Now the boy stood over his fallen friend. By this point the father was muttering under his breath as he cut out chunks of meat for them to eat and to take to town to sell. You could tell that the father was agitated and that worried the boy. He didn't need his father getting even angrier. That would make the rest of the evening even worse than what it was going to be. The boy knew already that he was going to have to eat his friend and he didn't want to have to get a beating on top of it.

"Ok boy all done, this is going to be some good pig. Give the rest to his brothers and sisters over there. And if I see you talking to even one of them fucking things

I'll make sure everything that you like ends up as dead as your mama."

The boy did as he was told even no matter how wrong it really was to feed him to them. At the same time, the father walked the meat to the house to start cooking. The boy stood there and watched as the pigs ate up their brother. He couldn't take it anymore and started sobbing. He watched for his father at the same time and started to walk down the hill side by the creek and sit.

The boy loved coming down here and sitting. He could sneak away a lot of the times without his father yelling at him for doing it. To his father it must have been the peace the boy was looking for. Plus, what could the boy do really but sit and watch the low laying water slowly flow down out of sight.

As he sat there he would day dream. Today though he sat there and cried about his fallen friend and what had happened not moments ago. He thought about the friend sitting up in piggy heaven with his other friends that had been slaughtered by the hands of his father. He imagined them all rolling around and playing in a giant pig pen. He could even hear them. He could hear them talking to him as if he were there. Telling him that they were ok, and the boy telling them how sorry he was that they had to die like that. He sat there thinking about this for the longest time. He even thought about running beside them and playing with them in the fields.

Reality though, snuck back in though as his father was calling for him to eat. It took everything he had in him to say goodbye to his friend and begin the walk back up the hillside to the old paint less house.

The house and everything on the property wasn't really anything to look at. The property and its buildings had run itself down after the boy's mother had died. It used to be a beautiful house painted white with a red barn.

11

There were yellow flowers planted around the front of the house and hanging baskets of flowers hanging off the ceiling of the porch. Everything had its place when she was alive. The animals all had clean pens to live in and horses roamed the fields alongside crops, so the boy was told.

All of that was gone now. Ten years later and his father left all of it go. The father never bothered to lift a paint brush again. He still grows crops, but the horses were sold. The pig pens and the roof of the barn is barley on. The flowers died off the first winter of her being gone and the roof of the porch blew off the same year due to a blizzard.

The boy walked inside. There was beautiful hard wood everything in the house, but the boy never seen that version of the house. Now the floor was rubbed down without varnish. The walls were tar yellow from the cigarettes his father smoked. The flower curtains were no longer in the windows. Beer bottles stacked the floor and many stands didn't make it from his father's drunken smash sessions. Each can have had cigarette butts or chew spit in each of them. There was also a fire place in the living room with a very nice wooden mantle. The fire place was the only place that was clean. It had the boy's mother's ashes on it. The father was only faithful to cleaning the mantle because of her ashes. It was the only thing he cared about.

In the dining room slash kitchen was as bad as the living room which was separated by a half wall so you could see into the living room. The only exception was the dishes were cleaned everyday by the boy. The table had two small clearings for them to eat at. The stove had built up grease that was so bad that it couldn't be scrapped off. The refrigerator had mold and a very foul smell in it. The freezer was frozen shut and couldn't even be open. So, when they killed something to eat, they ate for the next week and maybe even longer even though it made him sick every time.

The boy sat down in his chair with a plate of his friend waiting. He sat and stared at the ham. Tears filled his eyes. He wondered how his father could make him do this. He didn't want to eat the only living thing ever to be known to him as a friend. What was he too do though? If he refused he wouldn't eat for a week because father would not let him eat until he agreed to eat his friend. Also, the boy was terrified of the beating he would receive. Last time he received a beating he could barely walk after. It took three weeks before he did walk without a limp.

"What's the matter boy? You had better eat that. I worked real hard to put your little friend on that plate for you." The father said all of this with a smirk on his face and laughing at the end as if he enjoyed torturing his only son. He leaned back in his chair and lit a cigarette and took

14

a large drink of beer out of the bottle with smoke coming out of his nose and mouth as he sat down the bottle.

The boy looked down at the ham on the plate and picked up the knife and fork. The father didn't make anything else with the meal, so the boy couldn't stall anymore. With fork and knife clinched in his hands lying on the table a few tears fell out of the boy's eyes and hit the table.

"Are you fucking crying? You need to be a man! Stop fucking crying, baby! With those words spoken the father reached across the table and slapped the boy as a hard as he could on the left side of his head. The blow was so hard it knocked him down to the dirty floor. The father got up from his chair and picked him up off the ground with his hands around his neck.

"BOY! You better stop crying and eat." The father slammed down the boy back in his chair. The father stood over top of the boy with one hand on the back of his neck and the other beside the plate.

"Eat it." He said over and over but the boy didn't budge. He continued to cry. The father got down face level with the crying boy. He starred for a time at the boy. The boy just sat there crying and shaking scared what was going to happen next.

The father reached over to the plate and picked up the meat. Still staring at the boy intensely the father began circling his thump on the meat. Breathing harder and harder, the anger on the face of the father grew as he slowly lifted the hand with the meat in it. The boy tried to push back but couldn't, the other hand of the fathers kept pushing towards the meat hand. The boy really started to cry with his lips quivering in fear. He knew it was to the point where he had no choice but to eat. If he resisted his father would shove the meat down his throat and get beaten even more. If he went with the eating of the meat

16

he might live to see tomorrow. The beatings were never bad enough that the boy thought he might die, but tonight he thought it was possible. There was something special to this night. His father had something extra in his anger. It was very odd and the boy had no clue as to what it was.

The boy leaned over took the hardest bite of food of his life. The father let go of his backside when he bites into the meat. The father stood up and went back to his side of the very small round table and opened another beer. He just sat there in the same angered look as before smoking another cigarette.

"Fuck boy, when are you ever going to learn to be a man? You can't keep up this teary-eyed bullshit up forever. I wish you had died instead. I lose your mother for you? That isn't fucking right. Ten fucking years ago today she passes and she left me with a little girl."

Chapter 2

It had been 10 years ago today that the boy's mother had died. The problem was that it was also the boy's birthday. His mother had died while giving birth, but the he was saved. At first the father was a normal man in that situation. He grieved hard. The child brought him joy at first. He even had his now late mother move in with him to help him. Nothing was really the same for him though. The love of his life had passed on to the other side and he was stuck on earth without her.

For a few years things went ok but you could see the downward spiral of the father's sanity slowly going downhill. He started yelling at his mother and yelling at the young boy. The boy looked just like his mother and that just turned the stomach of his father. Instead of being reminded of her in a good way, all he seen was a murderer. From then until now the boy never received a name from anyone, he was just called Boy. In fact, to this day the birth certificate only has boy on it.

After few years of his mother helping she decided she had enough of the father's insensitivity for the boy. She demanded that he give him a proper name, not boy. They would argue, even to the point of who should even take care of him. The father refused to do anything for the boy or even talk to him unless he had too.

One day in the evening the father and his mother started fighting with each other and began to become the loudest fight ever between the two. The boy came to the aid of his grandmother and put himself between the middle of the two. During the fight, the boy was shoved into the grandmother knocking her over smashing her head into an end stand. She took rest in the boy's room for a few days and ended passing away. The father buried her himself behind the house. This would become off limits to the boy and his father would never step foot back there again.

Now it has been ten years since the no named boy's mother had died and his grandmother had died only two years ago. Now all he had left was his father. The boy didn't believe that his father didn't love him. He just wanted to make him suffer for causing two deaths. The boy seemed to be ok with that too, because that had been his life up until now, punishment for death that he has caused.

The boy never new when his birthday was, but that also means that was the day his mother died too. They never celebrated the birthday. He didn't even know his exact age was until today. To the boy his father had just opened up to him. He wanted to smile and thank his father for slipping the information, but his father did say he wished he was dead. So, the boy just sat there eating his friend. With the mixed emotions, he just sat there staring at his father. His head was throbbing from the blow to the head, but the boy ignored the pain. The father sat there looking down at the table smoking, drinking, and eating.

The two didn't say anything to each other except when the boy was ordered to bed. This was his favorite time of the day for the boy. They had no television and the boy couldn't read that much since the father keeps him from schools. The boy would lay in bed and day dream about the future, about leaving the farm. He would lay there and think about how his life would be different if his mother and grandmother where alive and how his father would act if they were.

The boy laid there tonight wondering specifically about his birthday and had forgotten the pig slaughter that had happened earlier. He wondered what his mother even looked like because his father had burned pictures of her before the boy could ever get to see them

Laying and wondering eventually brought the boy to sleep. During his sleep, he had a dream. The dreamed involved a woman he never met. She came out of the fields by the creek. With long red hair pale white skin dressed in a light blue thin dress, the woman would come and sit down beside him.

"Hello son. I'm your mother. I have been watching you for a long time now. I am always around watching. I know that you have things hard right now but one-day things will change. You will grow big and turn into a man. For now, though you need to continue what you are doing and figuring things out with life and the farm. The lines will start to intertwine and you will figure out that death is a normal part of life and also with farming. Your father is getting you ready for many things, things that he doesn't even know about yet. One day this will all make sense and you will have the friends you want and then some. Then I'll be back to guide you to the next part of life. Just remember I am always with you, watching, and that I love you."

The next morning the boy was awakened by his father screaming for him to get up and start his morning chores. During the day, the boy thought and thought of the dream, none of it seemed right though. He wondered about what his father would do or say about the dream if he knew about it.

Later in the day his father went in the house to begin his usual drinking. When he did, the boy went down to the creek and lay on the side of the hill. He wished his mother would appear like in the dream, but nothing happened. Maybe it was just a dream the boy thought, but it seemed so real. The boy ran the dream back threw his mind and tried to remember every little detail.

What did his mother mean by saying she would always be around? The dream had been confusing enough, maybe it didn't mean anything. The boy laid there for some time, waiting for the normal drunken screaming and possible beating his father was about to give him. His mother had told him that his father was getting him ready for the future, but no matter how much he wanted to believe his mother, he just couldn't bring himself to believe that.

The yelling had begun in the back ground, from the house. The boy got up and walked himself up the hill to the house. Silent and calm was the standard as always. The boy never wavered from this behavior. He feared that if he should show any emotion that his father would be even harder on him like the night before. The father could come to realize that underneath his exterior that he was being soft on the boy and then he would have beat him worse and worse to prove he wasn't soft. This was to be the reasoning for the boy being silent and emotionless most of the time.

CHAPTER 3

For the next few years the boy walked around the farm doing his chores. He learned a lot about the farm and the reasons behind everything done. The boy and his father didn't grow close during this time either. The father stayed stern on being forceful and striving to make his son survive a living hell. The father continuously beat and yelled at his son. The boy always took the beatings and never fought back.

Over the years the boy began to learn to withdraw himself away from the farm and daydream about other worlds and his mother. His mother hadn't been back since that faithful night a few years back. The boy had even begun to let the memory of the dream fade from his mind. Thinking that the mother would never come back like she said, he also started doubting that she was around all the time like she said.

After the pig was killed a few years ago, the boy learned to disconnect himself with all living things. Things had become so mundane for him that killing had become a normal way of life for him. Never did he want this. It had just started to grow on him. The thought of any living thing having a soul had become lost in his mind. There was no anger there, there wasn't love there, and there was no emotion for the animals anymore.

Just like the animals, any love for his father had become lost completely. The saying, you will love your family no matter what, was not true in this case. In some sick way, his father seemed to be right when he made the boy kill the pig. It's a part of life on the farm. Unfortunately, he learned not to love anything at all. The boy didn't try to attempt any connection with anything anymore. Not even for a dream with his mother in it.

The beatings had slowed down though. The boy started to do as he was told and learned to sneak away in

26

his head and pay attention at the same time. The father was none the wiser. That doesn't mean the father was nicer to the boy or anything like that, he still hated his son for killing his wife. Though, the father had started to pick up local whores from the town near the farm. He would drive to the town on a Friday evening and pick up the cheapest he could afford and bring her home for the weekend.

The women would stay and they would get drunk and have wild sex parties around the house. There was no discretion either. If they wanted to have sex when the boy was around, then it would happen and the boy would leave. He showed no interest in the women his father brought home. For a teenage boy, not to show any interest in the female body was odd, but the disconnection of emotion and physical attraction had been taken away from the boy. The father though finally gave into the fact that the mother was never coming back and went out and found a solution to his loneliness.

You would think that this would make the father nicer, possibly calm him down some. No chance. The father moved faster and hit harder. He could do what he wanted when he wanted. If the women of the weekend mouthed off he would hit them too. They were so far from town that walking was out of question. The women would get scared sometimes being out there in nowhere, they would freak out. Then the father would hit or even force himself on the women if they had second thoughts. This had become paradise for the father. His own personal kingdom, any woman he wanted, and a personal slave also the heir to his thrown.

The boy could hear things heating up on the weekends threw his paper-thin walls. He could fear the flesh hitting flesh, either via sex or the father slapping the women. It had become a new routine for this family of a father and a son. So much so the boy had become accustomed to these things that happened. If they didn't happen then something was wrong and a severe beating would be headed his way.

The boy inside hadn't completely fallen to his father's kingdom. The boy still had his mind. He still could escape to that place that not even his father could touch. On the nights when the sex had become loud and violent, then boy would sneak down to the creek. There the boy would lie in the grass and listen to the water trickle. The boy would think about what the rest of the world was like. He never had really been out of the farm since he had been little. His father would only take him to town occasionally.

While he was in the city he would watch people and the interaction between them. He never knew what being nice and loving was like. He didn't comprehend the differences between them with his father anymore. He knew for years why he hated him so much, the death of his mother. These people would laugh and enjoy themselves.

They weren't even drunk, like his father had to be to do it. He never saw anyone else being hit or yelled at.

He would put himself there. In his head, he would travel the long road to town and interact with people. The boy would join his made-up family and friends for dinner and then go to a movie. He had never actually been to a movie though. He knew what they were, but never seen one. Once he saw a television in a store front window, which caused a pause that landed him a beating when he was home.

Interaction with his father was what he wanted at the beginning of his life, but almost sixteen years into his life he didn't care anymore. A cold dark hard life was ahead of him and his father was the slave master. With little hope still left in his heart regained from lying on the grass by the creek he would sneak back into his room hoping not to get caught or to hear the sexual perversions his father and his companion for that night.

Once in his room he would lay there until his father would come in and wake him. The boy rarely slept. He always kept his mind focused which made him sleep deprived. If he slept he would lose focus, which would make him slip up and get a beating. His only sanity that was left was the escape he could rescue from in the deep thoughts of normalcy that was lodged in his mind.

CHAPTER 4

"Wake up Boy. Time to get your shit over with. You little crumb snatching fuck, get up!"

Another morning of waking up to his father's usual hurtful remarks and the boy continued to keep silent. Not a peep. He would get out of bed get dressed and begin work. Life had become routine at the farm. The boy and his father would go different ways to get the work done faster now. One would handle cleaning and feeding and the other killing and butchering.

For a two-man operation the father was making above normal amounts of money. It wasn't a great amount, but it got him everything he wanted. It didn't matter what the boy wanted though, he was never asked. Plus, how else would he be able to pay for the women that he brought home. Food and sex had become the life of the father. No woman really liked the man that much either.

Today though was different. It was almost an evaluation day at work. The father decided he was going to follow the boy around all day to make sure everything was going well. He didn't want to lose profit.

He followed his son up and down feeding then watched as he cleaned the pens. He didn't lift a finger the whole time either. The father just stood and watched. It had almost been six years since the faithful day the pig friend was killed, and today the father was going to really push for some butchering.

"Okay Boy, let's kill us some pigs." The father said chuckling. "I don't want you to do it humane either; I want you to see their souls leave."

The boy just glared at his father. Anger filled every ounce of his body, but did as he was told. With it being six years later and the boy becoming a young man, he had become very muscular and didn't need much help anymore.

"Come on fucker, I want you to get eye to eye with that swine and cut its fucking throat open, just like it was a person."

The boy just stood there. He didn't want to do it. The beating would come if he didn't, but he had grown used to the beatings. The fists didn't bother him; it was when he used weapons that hurt or got kicked. Anything he could grab, he would use. Last year he even got stabbed a few times with forks. Those really hurt badly.

The boy decided to get done what needed to be done. The boy then crouched down and looked the pig right in the eyes. Next, he reached back and shoved the knife right up into the throat of the pig. The pig tried to get away but the knife held him there. The boy stared at eyes of the pig as blood ran down his arms and legs. The eyes of the pig showed the boy death close and personal as its eyes turned milky white. He could see the soul of the pig backing away and vanishing. The boy felt empowered by the killing of the pig. He felt full of energy. The body continued to twitch, but the pig had died.

The father had finally had his son do what he originally wanted him to do years ago. He wanted the boy to see the soul leave the body just like he watched his wife's soul vanish from her eyes.

The boy picked up the dead pig and moved him to the slaughter table and began to cut up the pig. He had no emotion on his face, neither did the father as he walked away to continue his work on another part of the farm. The evaluation was over.

The cutting of the pig didn't bring any emotion to the boy. It was almost as if there was nothing left inside. The waiting for his mother to come back in a dream had disappeared. The hopes of his father ever excepting him had gone. The dream of one day leaving the farm behind still lingered with little light and was burning out. The boy was slowly becoming his father.

Later that night the boy went to bed without a beating. He did everything correctly almost militant like. For the first time ever the father even gave a smirk of approval of his son. Though the boy didn't take it and shrugged it off as he knew it meant nothing.

CHAPTER 5

His son, it wasn't something the father had ever thought of before. He never looked at this child as his own flesh and blood. It was a creation he helped make with his departed wife. He held a grudge for so long, that he had suppressed the idea that his wife and he had shared this together. They painted the boy's bedroom and had bought him toys. These things didn't last after her death, but the father seen himself in his child today, and in an odd way was proud of the boy for killing the pig.

Forgiveness though was out of the question though. There may be a small possibility of acceptance though, and it would be a start. The man decided he was going to start taking the boy to town with him more often to show him more of the family business. It wasn't a present that the boy would enjoy. The boy didn't care about the family business. He never thought of it more than farming, killing, selling, eating, and his father's whores. The boy would take the ride though. He had rarely seen the outside lands of the farm. He would take what he would get at this point. With little emotion left inside he became excited when they would reach the town. They always drove straight to the butcher's shop and drop off the latest kill.

Today though, today was different. The father had bigger plans. They did the stop at the butchers and then went the grocers. The father told the boy to wait in the truck while he went in. The boy sat there as instructed. He sat and people watched. He watched families interacting with each other and couples playfully kissing. He seen children running threw a nearby park playing with each other. The boy stayed emotionless though. He just studied everyone. He didn't wonder about where they worked or the love they felt for each other, but the how. How everything worked. How did this person react when the other person did something? The intimate details of the kissing of the couple sitting on a bench, and the wonder of how kids could interact and be playful.

By this point sometime had passed and the father finally came out followed by a woman. The woman looked like a worker at the grocers. She was an average looking woman, with the average look that he was used of being seen from his father's whores. When they arrived at the truck, the boy was ordered to the bed truck. He had no problem with that, he was able to watch the wonder of the openness of open movement. It was like riding in a cheap convertible. The boy had never sat in the back like this before. There was a sense of freedom that never had been there before. He sat and watched nature and buildings pass by as if going one hundred miles per hour when only doing about forty. There was something magical that was happening to the boy, he started growing emotion inside of him. He started to feel emotion towards his father for the first time since he was little.

The feelings that the boy felt inside was mixed though. On one hand, he felt happy that his father may be recognizing him as a person and possibly his son. On the other hand, though, there was anger and rage. Why hadn't his father ever taken him to the town more often with him? Why was his father treating him like this? It had never happened before. Was it because of the pig? The slaughter of the animal had hardened him. His whole life was about hardening and discipline. Was this the time for them to move forward?

As they pulled in to the long-hidden drive way that would take them through trees and more trees to the end. They were back at the house where discipline ruled the kingdom. The boy stopped the emotional thoughts that had been going through his head. It was if a light switch turned on in his head and whipped clean any thought of normalcy of life. This had been an emotion that he would wash away from memory, because the thought of what he wanted life to be would end up probably killing him.

When they arrived, the boy knew not to follow to the house because of what his father and the woman were going to do. He didn't completely understand the world of

sex and the skin of another person, other than he knew

where babies came from. It's the only thing that he knew.

There was still no curiosity in it with him though. Militant

was his way as he went and started to work on his chores

for the evening.

CHAPTER 6

As the evening grew darker and darker that night, the sounds of the relations from the old farm house grew louder and louder. The boy tried to do whatever he had to do to stay away until the noise subsided. He spent a good portion of the evening sitting by the stream and watching nature push the water down past his eye sight. Watching the waters movement had increasingly becoming increasingly his way of suppressing and staying focused. He just stared for hours at how the water would pass over rocks and tree limbs. He never thought of a supreme being doing any of this because it was something that left the home with his grandmother and he couldn't remember any of the teachings that had been taught to him these many years later. He never asked the whys to these things, he just knew that water ran on a downgrade. He knew that crops grew and that they were cut to be ate and sold. He knew animals were breed and ate. The morals to all the things that made him were just the militant like way of life. The only moral rule he knew was not to piss off his father. It was his way or the beating way. It was the only thing he knew of anything.

The sexual noises subsided from the house as the boy had been hoping they would so he could eat. He walked himself up to the old beat up house that was really at its worst in years. It was always bad but the roof now leaked and the heat rarely worked. Most of the windows were broken and the door didn't always latch itself anymore.

The boy walked through the doorway of the house and avoided his eyes away from his father and his female friend of the night. His father sat in his chair in his underwear smoking a cigarette. He only ever smoked a cigarette after the relations had been completed. The woman lay on the couch with a sheet barely covering her naked body. She laid there smoking a cigarette with a smirk, almost smile on her face. The sheet was almost see threw, but the women brought home didn't seem to care about the modesty. Most women would try to cover up more, but the father would make the women continue going on with what she was doing when the boy walked in. If the woman was straddling the father during intercourse he would make them continue, or if the woman was performing oral on him he would just hold down their head so they couldn't stop. Without ever watching, the boy knew everything about how women looked naked and how everything worked with intercourse, but he always tried to avoid the sight of his father with a woman. To this point in the boy's life this is all he knew of women and didn't really think that they had been put on the earth for much more. Just like when animals have intercourse, it is just animal instinct, so that's what the boy thought of intercourse, to reproduce.

The couch had been turned since years past; it was with the same wall as the door, so the boy could avoid his eyes from the women lying on the couch. The chair his father was sitting in was facing the dining room and kitchen area though. The father watched as his son walk in and head for the kitchen. The half wall that separated the two areas had become beaten up so badly that there were just a few studs still holding it up. Over the years his father had either put his fist or foot threw the wall. Even worse was when he would slam the boy up against the wall. Then there were the few times he would throw women against it after they had pissed him off. Those women had to walk back to town. Most likely thumbing a ride once they reached the main road.

"Cook all three of us some food boy."

The son did as he was told. He fried up some ham and mashed up some potatoes for the three of them. This puzzled the boy though. The father never had him cook for a woman. The boy never cooked for his father on the nights that a female was there. The boy started to wonder if it was a possible replacement for his mother finally. It was a long shot, but there were too many things that were going on today that was too odd not to think of such things. Imagine a mother, the boy thought, someone that could possibly change things here. Maybe the father would be less mean. Maybe the father could loosen the militant noose that hung around his neck.

The father removed himself from his chair and went out and sat at the table. The woman stood up carelessly removed the sheet exposing himself to the boy and then wrapping it around her like a towel. While she was doing this the boy turned his back to the woman as if he were engrossed in his cooking. When he turned around the women sat down at one of the chairs carelessly spreading her legs apart a little and letting the sheet fall down her chest to where her nipples were the only thing holding up the sheet. The boy had seen her exposure and looked straight to the floor trying not to look. The woman giggled a little when she noticed the boy doing this and confused it for politeness.

"Boy, this is Lucy. Get used of seeing her. Things around here are going to change for now on."

Was it what the boy had thought? The boy smiled on the inside. Something that was rare on the inside as well as on the outside, but he didn't want his father to know what he had hoped for. Could this woman, Lucy be his new mother? He looked Lucy in the eyes to really look at her as they ate. Lucy just smiled and looked back at the boy. As she moved around eating and talking with his father the sheet began to fall off her chest. The boy glanced as it happened and looked away right away.

Lucy giggled at the boy. "They're just boob's kid. You know tits? Don't tell me you have never seen them before." She smiled bigger and bigger as she spoke. "It's ok, I don't mind if you look."

"You heard her Boy, you better look. I swear as much pussy as I have had in here, I never once caught him looking; I think he's a fucking queer. Are you a fag Boy?

Is that what it is" The fathers voice grew louder and louder

as he spoke. Lucy's smile went away as he slammed his

fist against the table looking for answers. The father stood

up leaning across the table over into the face of his son.

Lucy began to back up a little and started to cover herself

up a little.

"Take that sheet off Lucy."

"Jim I'm not sure what's going on here, you're

scaring me."

The father ripped the sheet off Lucy exposing her

to the boy. Next, he walked around the table to the boy.

Lucy sitting there as she began to shake, not from being

cold but from the fear of what might happen next to her.

The father grabbed the back of the boy's neck, leaned

down next to the boy's ear, and talked softly.

"Boy, there is pussy right in front of you, and you won't look. LOOK!" He screamed in the ear of his son. "Spread your fucking legs women!" She did slowly looking up at the ceiling with a few tears coming down her cheeks. The man stared a whole in the side of the boy's head. He was looking as instructed. He seen how Lucy was growing uncomfortable with the situation, but what the boy didn't know was that she was here for him, not his father. The father pushed his son to the floor and dragged him in front of Lucy. She moved her herself to the end of the chair without instruction. The father than shoved his sons face into Lucy's vagina, moving his head back and forth, repeatedly, in and out.

"Stick out your tongue out fag! Come on eat that pussy!" The father said with a mean, stern, laugh.

"Jim, let us go to his room, please. I can't do it like this. Let us do this alone, please."

"Fine, but you better fuck him. I'm not paying you to be his mother!"

Lucy stood up and grabbed the boys hand and helped him up off the ground. She then led him to his room and laid him on his back on the beaten-up thing that was his bed.

"It's ok, I'll take care of you, and you don't have to worry about anything. It's actually really cool of a dad to get his son laid." Lucy said with a smile. She sat sown beside the boy who still had shown any emotion. The dream of this being his new mother had been shattered to pieces fast, very fast. He knew the mechanics to all of this from watching the farm animals, but he didn't know he was old enough to breed yet."

Sitting next to him, Lucy started rubbing on his pants where his penis was. She began to stroke him threw the jeans a little bit. She then unbuttoned and unzipped his pants and pulled them back a little to expose the boy's penis. It had become erect, which was something new for him. Yes, he did get an erection occasionally, but never knew you could get it from stroking it.

"Ah there you go; I knew you had it in you. I know you probably don't know anything about what is going to happen or feel, but that's okay, we have all night to do this. You're going to cum big and fast the first time, and then we will really play after that."

Lucy then lowered her head and placed his penis in her mouth. She stroked the penis fast and ran her tongue back and forth on the underside of the head of the penis. It didn't take long, just like she said. The boy started to feel things that he had never felt before, his body began to tingle. His penis became harder and harder until it felt like all life inside of him exploded into the mouth of Lucy.

With his toes curled and his legs stiffened, Lucy sat up opened her mouth to show the boy what he had deposited in her mouth and then swallowed it all. She then proceeded to lean back over and began to suck on his penis again to get the rest out and to keep his penis hard. When she was satisfied that he would stay hard for her she straddled him and began to ride him.

All the emotions and chemicals that were being released inside the boy, he could hardly think straight. He knew what was going on but didn't understand why she swallowed his seed. Now with her on top of him ridding him, thrusting, and wiggling back and forth the boy couldn't come up with any reasoning of why him and now. He really loved how the warmth of being inside her felt, but knew that she wasn't here for his seed to reproduce like the rest of the animals do. Then before he knew it the feeling overcame the thought and released again inside Lucy's vagina. This he knew was to be more natural. She then rolled off him gave him a kiss on the lips and told him thank you and walked out.

That was it. It was over. The boy laid there with his father walking up to the doorway and peeking in seeing his half naked son laying there with a still erect penis. The father turned around and walked out shutting the door behind him. The boy could hear them talking from his room. He could hear them talk about how she had the boy, and what she did with his sperm. The father was not happy when he found out that he had ejaculated in her. It ruined her for him, so he slapped her across the face knocking her to the ground where he kicked her in the stomach, all could be heard by the boy.

The boy stood up and put on his pants and peered out the doorway to watch him beat on Lucy. He kept screaming at her for being careless and what if the boy got her pregnant? So, he would kick her in the stomach again. She laid there crying and begging for him to stop, but he wouldn't. He grabbed her by the back of the hair and

dragged her over to the chair and lifted her up on it so that

her behind was sticking up in the air from the elbow rests.

The father than pulled out his penis and forced himself

into the anal cavity of Lucy. She screamed and the father

smiled. The boy watched from the door. He didn't know

what to do, Lucy was nice to him, but if he interfered with

what was going on than the boy would get a beating. The

boy was confused. He didn't know if this was normal or if

it wasn't. The boy would step out and then step back into

his room, pacing. Everything the boy had ever learned was

being thrown around in his head. He knew his father was

not a good man. He knew that humans were nothing more

than animals. Lucy was being treated like an animal, but

animals don't scream in pain and his father was not trying

to reproduce like an animal. Neither did Lucy earlier with

the boy. The boy was lost and his head was spinning with

unanswered questions and thoughts and then the crying

stopped. Everything halted to a whimper as his father

pulled himself out of Lucy. Lucy tried to get up but his

father punched and knocked her out. The father laughed a little as he grabbed another cigarette and walked around and sat himself in the chair. As he sat there he smoked and stroked himself, flinging his penis forward to get the rest of the sperm to come out and let it fall on the floor.

CHAPTER 7

The following day the boy went and did his daily chores. There laid Lucy who was bruised very badly. Blood had dried around her nose and on the floor where she was passed out. The father was on the couch passed out from all the alcohol that he had drank the night before. This was nothing unusual though, but not everything about last night was normal though. The boy who never even masturbated before had sex. This was completely new to the boy, and he liked it. He now understood why his father would invest money so these women would stay for the weekend or longer and spend having intercourse with him. The confusion came though when the boy couldn't understand that intercourse was to be done for reproduction like an animal, but it wasn't being done for that. He enjoyed the sex, but it wasn't right. His father had stopped the act of pregnancy from happening and so did she. She swallowed the boy's seed; he knew that wasn't right either.

Many things were going through the head of the boy as he did his chores. He was making decisions on life that were based off farm animals. He didn't realize that humans were superior to the farm animals. Humans to him were equal to the animals he took care of and then slaughtered for food. He seen animals give birth and die only to watch the young live, just like him and his mother. Animals mating were nothing new to him either. Penis inserted to vagina and then they would have intercourse and then most of the time the animal would then give birth. This had never happened though when his father brought home one of his women for the weekend, or at least he had never seen any other children.

With these questions there were no answers. He had no one to talk to. He had no television to watch. There were no books in the house hold. There was the occasional nudie magazine lying around, but the boy never picked them up. He never knew there was anything for him to be interested in when it came to women. He never guessed that his father would bring home a woman for him to have intercourse with. This was something nice his father had done. It had slipped his mind. His father maybe was changing. Things wouldn't be clear until later, but for now the boy had a small ray of hope, possible change in his life. When he thought of how this ray of hope was created, the ray was through the slaughter of an animal. Was that right? He wasn't sure. Did he even want the approval or love from his father? Killing the animals seemed easy enough. He always watched his father do it without any display of emotion when having to kill, and that's what he displayed the day before emotionless connection to an animal. The slaughter of the animal and the boy did not feel any remorse. Watching the soul leaving the eyes of the animal was empowering even. It almost fed the boy inside in an emotional place that needed to be fed.

Watching the soul slip away from the body of the animal changed the insides of the boy. It empowered him with the taking of something that can't be touched any other way. He started feeling something on the inside, almost the urge to kill another animal again. He looked around at all the animals that were there. There was another pig that was due soon and the boy couldn't wait. He wanted to kill the pig in another way than he has watched his father do, and in another way than what he had done. He wanted to watch the life drain in the eyes again. The cloudiness that washed over the eyes can never be forgotten.

All in about a forty-eight-hour period the boy learned that there were two things driving him now. There was the thrill of killing an animal and the unbelievable passion that he had experienced only a few hours ago. His chores were almost complete when he saw his father walking out of the house. The father stumbled down the beaten road to the barn where the boy stood. The stood there with a militant stance as always, waiting for orders. The father walked right past him and began to work like always. The boy wanted to talk to his father about the night before, but didn't know how to go about it. There was the small problem also; the boy never spoke, ever. If he spoke for the first time he didn't know how his father would act.

"Boy, go up to the house and check on Lucy. She probably still is pretty out of it. I gave her some pills so we could get a couple more fucks out of her. I already went once this morning. Put this on your dick and just stick it in the bitch."

The boy walked up to the house like his father told him to do. On the way, he read the side of the condom package that his father gave him. When he walked into the house Lucy was trying to move around crawling on the floor mumbling incoherent words. She crawled to the boy and sat in front of him unzipping his fly on his jeans.

"If I suck your dick, will you help me get out of here please?" Lucy said as she put his penis in her mouth without waiting for a response. The boy stood there for a moment and enjoyed the oral sex when he pulled back. He stood there and looked down at Lucy with tears coming down her cheeks. "Please."

The boy stepped back and grabbed Lucy by the arms and stood her up and looked at her straight in the eyes. He looked deep inside and seen fear inside them. The soul was torn and horrified at the things that had happened to her. The power of the soul being moved was a new thing. He didn't know that the soul could show emotion. Not only could he see the soul leave, but he could see what the soul felt as he peered into Lucy's eyes.

He looked at Lucy with a smile. Then Lucy smiled. He watched the fear go away in the eyes in Lucy and the soul changed to hope that the ordeal was over. The boy then threw Lucy down just onto the couch. She laid there and looked at the boy in fear again as he stripped naked and put the condom on his now very erect penis. Lucy tried to scream but the drugs didn't allow for her to get much sound out. The boy climbed on top of Lucy as she tried to squirm away but couldn't. The boy looked at Lucy right in the eyes as he forced himself into Lucy. Lucy tried to hit the boy, but he grabbed both her wrists with one hand and pushed them above her head. The boy began to thrust himself over and over again into Lucy. She began to cry and she closed her eyes. The boy grabbed her palming her face and using his fingers to open up one eye. Her eye showed fear and hate which fueled the boy. He watched the soul and the eye move all over. He continued to thrust and thrust until he was done. The boy lay on top of Lucy considering that one eye and watching all the different emotions run through her eye.

The boy crawled off Lucy who in turn curled up into the fetal position and started crying. He sat there and watched her as she laid there tormented from the weekend. There was a smile on his face as he stood up and walked in front of Lucy naked with the condom still on his now shrinking not so erect penis. He stood there looking down at her and pulled off the condom and looked at it. His seed was in the condom. He didn't understand that the sperm was to stay inside the condom. This meant his father sent him up for pleasure and not to breed. The boy stood there and wondered if that meant it was okay to just have pleasure? Under the circumstances that would indicate yes. The boy wasn't sure though, so he grabbed Lucy's legs and spread them and tried to stick the condom inside Lucy.

"You fucking idiot throw that away! You and your father are going to pay for all of this your sick fucks!" Lucy kicked at the boy and hit him the nuts and sent the boy to the ground. This angered him and he threw the condom into the face of Lucy. She shrieked as she ripped off the condom that now dripped sperm all over her and threw it over towards his father's chair.

The boy got up and dressed himself. He started to smile as he looked at Lucy. He felt the power of her soul

63

inside him and he knew that he had a piece of her now

inside. It made him feel stronger now than after he killed

the pig. Now he had collected two souls and it seemed to

feed a new lust that he never knew existed inside of him.

The boy loved the new emotion. He knew that he still

would have to be militant around his father, but he was ok

with this form of freedom that was created and he couldn't

wait for more souls.

CHAPTER 8

Lucy ended up staying around for longer than she was prepared for. She asked to leave the same morning the boy had forced himself on her. The father though convinced her to stay and take care of them for a longer period. He wanted her to serve them whenever they wanted. Lucy at first wasn't a fan of this concept, but ended up staying due to the thought of not having to work at all. All she would have to do is have sex. That seemed simple enough. She didn't have to go back to her old life and work for a living and being a hooker on the side for extra cash. There was free food and a roof over her head; she believed she couldn't go wrong.

The boy in this situation though became increasingly confused. He enjoyed the feminine touch that she provided, but there was that lack of reproduction. They were still not like the animals. They didn't have intercourse to make a baby, which still confused him. On

65

the other hand, he loved how everything felt. His penis inside her whenever he wanted and where ever he wanted was phenomenal to him. After a few days, even Lucy had become accustomed to whenever the boy walked up to her and opened his pants, pulled out his penis, and put it towards her mouth she would just suck on him until he was done.

A few weeks of sexual pleasure had gone past and nothing had changed. The father had even taken Lucy to go get her things from her home and move her in. She ended up moving into the father's room, but sleeping in the boy's room sometimes. The beatings seemed to be slowing down on the boy because the father started spending more time with Lucy and was less time focused on the boy. He started sending the boy to do more chores that the father had normally done himself. The boy didn't notice at first because he was getting to focus on killing animals. The pigs and every other animal were on the market now because the father was too busy with Lucy. He started dissecting any animal that he could catch. He skinned everything he caught as if it were a trophy to him. He would hang the furs up in the butcher's barn next to his special sharp knives that he personally started sharpening. Each knife had its place where it would be used in an animal.

The boy started to severally experiment with trying to keep the animals awake while he dissected them and almost had it down to a science. The tranquilizers he would use would be compared to the weight of the animal. He knew what he could cut and keep the animal alive. He knew how far he could take it before he would consider their eyes to watch the soul leave.

He started to wonder where the soul went increasingly. Every soul that passed seemed to bring him strength. There seemed to be power in killing these animals. As the cloudy look would cover the eyes, the boy could feel the life leave the animal and sink into his eyes.

The boy loved the empowerment, just as he loved the empowerment over Lucy. She though was becoming increasingly his father's woman rather than the animal that he had come to enjoy. Also, the father seemed to be doing less around the farm and seemed to become the boy's farm, not his father's anymore.

Thinking during a dissection of a rabbit that he had captured, the boy wondered if his father had hit a point where there was no more need for him. Had the father reached the point where he was to butcher, packaged and then sold? They had never done a human before, but they were just animals too. What about Lucy, she had basically stopped having intercourse with him, so there was no point in keeping her unless she started again. Still, the boy knew they didn't kill humans, but was it because they had never had a human before or was it that other people just took care of the butchering of humans?

By the end of the dissection of the rabbit the boy decided to leave things be for now. The father did help everyday still, and Lucy would give him oral still. The boy though was growing impatient with the situation and not knowing answers to his questions anymore. His mother had not come back to him in a dream at all since the first time and he had no one else to ask. There was the fact to that he wouldn't talk to anyone anyway. He had yet to ever speak. Groans and grunts while working and sexual encounters were the extent and the boy wasn't going to start now. The beatings had almost stopped and did stop in front of Lucy; he just didn't want to chance it. The father had started to use more weapons to beat the boy too. The boy had grown to a full-sized man and was ripped with muscles since he was a farm boy. The father hitting had started to weaken so he needed to use things that would hurt the boy, such as a baseball bat or other blunt objects. Though the father still knew how to make things painful when he took you to the ground, he didn't need a weapon then.

When dusk was starting to settle, the boy did his normal walk up to the house tired from doing all the work. Things once again had changed since Lucy moved in, there was food cooked for him every evening. He had started to be treated like the man of the house while the father almost is treated as the grandfather of the house. He played the all-knowing part and what he said was the word and gospel of the house. This night however was different, the father was not home. He had taken food to the town to be sold. That left Lucy and the boy alone in the house. The boy sat down at the table and Lucy served him chicken and mashed potatoes. She sat beside him putting her hand on his leg rubbing it while he ate. The boy, like every other man began to start to get an erection. Lucy smiled when she felt him starting to rise to the occasion. She sat there without a top on and short cut off shorts on. This was normal dress for her, mostly naked.

"Tonight, your father is bringing home two more women so we can play with them too. I think I may have to take care of you though before he gets home. I'm not sure if you're going to get to play with the other women. It's a shame though; the only pussy you know is mine. Maybe I can get your father to give you one of the extras so you can feel something different. For now, though we need to get out that nervous load out of you."

Lucy then moved under the table and opened the pants of the boy and starts performing oral on the boy's penis. She grabs the boy's hand gets him to feel her breast at the same time. This action sends the boy over the top and makes him ejaculate in her mouth in which she swallows and continues to lick him clean. She crawls out from under the table and walks into the bathroom and brushes her teeth not to leave anything there for his father.

After the boy was done eating he goes and takes a shower. In the shower, he can hear the truck coming up the driveway with the laughter of other women. The boy starts

to get excited. He continues with his shower as he can hear

talking and laughing coming from the other room when he

hears the bathroom door open. The shower curtain opens

slowly with a hand he doesn't know. It is a woman naked

standing there smiling. The woman has brown long hair

down to her behind and not a single hair anywhere else.

She is short with a big bust and a nice firm buttock from

what the boy can see. He also sees Lucy naked standing in

the doorway smiling.

"Do like her Boy? Your father gave you both of us

for a little bit while he takes care of Jan. He doesn't talk

ever Julie, so we just have to do things for him."

"What a fucking hot farm boy her Lucy, damn.

Why doesn't he talk?"

"I don't know, he won't say either."

Lucy walks up behind Julie presses herself against the body of Julie. She reaches around and starts messaging the breasts of Julie and kissing her neck. Julie slips her hands behind her and starts playing with Lucy's clit. Both women are groaning as the boy watches. Julie reaches out with one hand and runs her hand down the pecks of the boy down his abs to his erect penis.

"What should we do with him Lucy?' Moaning as she speaks.

"He's never had another woman; I want him to have you while I take care of myself and watch."

Julie turns and kisses Lucy feeling her breasts at the same time, then turns to the shower and gets in with him. She starts to kiss him and then moves to his neck. She continues down to the nipples and flicks and sucks it with her tongue. The boy moans and moans. He is enjoying everything. She gets on her knees and begins to give him oral with the shower water running over the two of them.

He looks over and sees Lucy watching them sitting against

a wall on the floor masturbating to the sight in front of her.

The boy is filled with emotions all great and wonderful,

empowering as Julie looks up at the boy as she continues.

He starts to get the power that emotion he gets from taking

souls and feels it as Julie is performing oral on his penis.

He reaches down and grabs a handful of hair and pulls her

up.

"Easy not so hard, you can pull but damn."

The boy pulls harder and looks in her eyes and she

pulls out a smile, and as he lifts her up puts himself inside

her. The boy places her on the side of the wall and thrusts

and thrusts. He starts throwing her around like a rag doll

changing positions. Julie is screaming from pleasure and

excitement which brings a smile to Lucy's face as she

ejaculates. The boy watched Lucy the whole time she was

ejaculating and locked eyes with each other. It empowered

the boy even more. Julie by this point had already received several enjoyments with the boy and her time in the shower with him. He then caries Julie out of the shower places her on the floor. The boy then grabs Lucy and makes her ride him while sitting on the toilet. At the same time Julie is making out with Lucy and kissing and licking her nipples and breasts. The boy reaches to the side of her head and makes her look him in the eyes. He makes her ride him harder and harder. He lowers his hands and reaches around her throat and squeezes a little bit. Julie sees this and puts her hands around the boys. Lucy is now thrusting as hard as she can as the oxygen gets slowly choked out of her. Julie pushes harder on the boy's throat. He can see the same look in the eyes in Lucy as he has the animals. She starts to gasp for air as tears rule down her checks, as she rips at his hands. Watching her slowly die makes him explode inside her. It was the best orgasm he ever experienced. His whole body tingled. He sat there with a smile on his face like he never had before. Lucy lied on the floor gasping for breath and trying to crawl up the wall to sit up right.

"I knew you guys were freaks out here, but fuck I never knew it was going to be this much fun." Julie said with a smile giggling. "I like it rough too. Want to fuck me again?"

The boy grabbed her by the hair and shoved her down in front of his penis which was still dripping from sperm and the fluids from Lucy. Julie began to lick his penis clean and performed oral sex on him again. Lucy lied on the floor and watched. She even started to play with her vagina and clit when the boy exploded in Julie's mouth. Julie leaned over to Lucy and kissed her giving her the sperm to swallow, which she did.

"We better shower and brush our teeth and get out there for Jim. Boy you better go off to bed. I think you have had enough for one day. Julie, I hope you saved some energy in case the old man has a lot."

The boy stood up and watched as both women went into the shower and washed themselves and had sex with each other. While he was watching instead of going to bed like he was told, he started to get aroused again, but decided to leave. He didn't need his father angry with him tonight; it had been too nice of a night for him to blow it.

CHAPTER 9

The next morning the boy awoke and began his normal chores. The boy had noticed that his father has been slower on his part of the work. In fact, a lot of the work had been being pushed onto the boy. The father was growing older and the boy was slowly becoming a man. In normal families, this would be a changing of the tides, but in the boys mind this was not how the world worked. The boy knew that when animals became too old they would be slaughtered and then made into food. This hasn't been done with humans though or at least they haven't done it to humans yet.

At what point the boy hadn't really noticed until this morning. This morning the father had taken extra time to get out on the tractor and moving onto work. It could have been from the four ways he had last night or father time was starting to talk to the father. The time of summer was winding down and it was time for the harvest to start, but the father was slowing down the process. The boy moved forward into his chores though. He had to slaughter another pig and another. The boy had become full time butcher of the farm. The meat was sold or ate at the farm.

Today the boy was extra angry about his life and the withering old father that was getting to ride along on a tractor while the boy had to kill. The boy was also tired from the night before but had more stamina. The killing had become mundane and didn't bother the boy anymore, unlike the first time he was made to kill a pig, a pig with a name that the boy loved. This thought started to loom in the boy's mind. The boy festered on the thought of the look of in the eyes of the pig as the life slipped out of them. He wondered if this was the same look that his mother had before she died. Was the look always the same? Was it the same animal to animal and human to human?

The boy looked out of the butchery to see if his father was far away on the field, and he was. With the doors closed and a pig waiting to be slaughtered, the boy began to look for something. Something that would slow down the pig and get eye to eye with the boy; it would have to be a different formula of tranquilizers. That would give him the results that the boy was curious about. The boy grabbed the needle and bottle and pulled the plunger back enough to slow down the pig, not to put it to sleep, or accidently kill it. With needle in hand the boy injected the pig in the neck. It was only a matter of minutes when the pig fell to its side.

Knife in hand the boy leaned over and looked the pig over. There was zero emotion in the boy. The boy had become so numb over time that nothing mattered anymore. Leaning closer to the pig he placed his ear to the chest of the pig to listen to its heart. It pounded with fear, almost like the animal knew what was about to happen, but not even the animal could be prepared for what was about to happen. The knife slide across the body of the animal not slicing it but just sliding it, still listening to the heart and how it began to beat harder out of fear, the boy leaned up and considered the eyes of the pig. They were the same look that the first pig had shown him. When the boy really thought about it, it was the look that all the pigs and other animals gave him. This was to be different though. With knife in hand the boy began to slice small incisions into the chest of the pig. The animal squealed in fear, it couldn't feel pain though because of the drugs. It knew something was wrong and that it shouldn't feel this way.

The boy began slowly cutting shapes out of the skin. It was slow like a surgeon. He was very meticulous in what he was doing. Cutting down the legs and peeling the skin off meat of the leg. The boy was seeing fear from the eyes of the pig as he continued his dissection of a living pig. There was a power that the boy had never felt before. A sense of control that he had never felt before in his life since everyone always told him what to do. The boy startled the pig and was looking down at the face of the pig as it cried in fear. With his knife, the boy began to cut to the center of the chest. Cutting a perfect line down the middle of it hitting bone, the rib cage, he had no tool for this. The boy looked around and found a hammer and a flat head screw driver. With the screw driver centered in the middle of the rib cage the boy hit it with the hammer cracking the bone. With a few hits, the boy had separated the rib cage and sat there watching the heart beating faster and faster with fear. He placed his hand on the heart; the life of the animal was literally in his hands. Considering the eyes of the animal and the animal looking back, the boy squeezed the heart and pulled as hard as he could, but it didn't come out. With the knife and a full angry thrust with the knife he cut it out.

Blood flooded out of the animal. It covered the entire floor of the barn. The boy sat still on top of the animal watching the eyes fade into the milky white look that all animals had had before this one. Sitting their heart in one hand and a knife in the other, he stood up and looked over the body of the animal. He stood there for a long time, letting the feeling of power wash over his blood-soaked clothes and body. To him it felt like he had captured the soul of the animal inside of him. The thought of this soul entering him and believing that the soul of the first pig was in him made him believe that this made him powerful. The boy that still lived inside also believed that his old friend had company finally after all these years and was happy. These feeling confused the boy but made him happy, and that was a rare thing for him.

He still didn't have much in his life. Work and sleep was still his primary things in life. Sex had come into his life, but the boy still didn't realize that it wasn't just for breeding, and that there should be pleasure associated with it. His father was growing older and older. The women that stayed in the house with them teased and belittled him when they wanted. None of them had become a mother figure that the boy needed the most. The boy had finally found something that made him happy. It was taking souls by looking in the windows of the animal.

For the next month, the animals that had to be slaughtered had to suffer through the soul collecting. Every day the boy would go to his chores with a new sense of purpose. He had started sloppy with the pig and began to clean up his act as he moved from one type of animal to another. Tools had to be modified to each specific situation and to each kind of animal. He would spend hours making new tools for different dissections. It wasn't about just the souls anymore, but how far could he keep the animal alive during the butchering. The boy started to believe that each animal that lasted longer than the other the stronger the soul and more power the boy would become, and he wanted as much as he could possibly have.

CHAPTER 10

It was morning on the farm and it was one of the days that the father would go into town and take meat to the store to sell and sometimes bring home a new woman for them to have sex with. Lucy still stayed at the farm and seemed to be a permanent member of the farm. On this morning, she was packing though. His father and she had a huge fight and she was looking to leave. She begged him to take her back to the city and that it was too long of a walk. The father pushed her away and grabbed her things and began throwing them outside telling her to start walking. The boy had become used to the arguments and the fights between the two, but then they would have sex and make up for a day or two. This time was different though, she never asked to leave before. Plus, the father was telling her to leave too. This was not a normal messed up morning that the boy had become used too. The father shoved Lucy to the floor and walked out and went to the truck. Lucy followed and tried to get to the truck before the father could leave but he was driving away by the time she hit the floor. The boy sat at the table staring at her.

"What the fuck are you looking at? I have to leave…" She said sarcastically. "I'm no good anymore. I'm wasted now. My pussy isn't good enough for you and your father anymore" Tears began coming down her eyes. "What am I supposed to do, huh?"

The boy sat there and thought for a few minutes and realized that she was old and no good to anyone on the farm and was all used up. The boy walked out to the barn where he did his dissections and grabbed the needle that had paralyzed every other animal. He then walked outside holding the needle behind him. Lucy was bent over picking up her clothes that the father had thrown everywhere. The boy walked up behind her and stood looking down on her.

"Well just don't just stand their freak, help me!" she screamed at him while crying. When she looked down at the ground again, the boy pulled the needle out and stabbed her in the side of the neck and pushed the plunger. She tried to stand up but she just stumbled and mumbled incoherent words to the boy as she fell straight to the ground. The boy leaned over and picked her up and began to carry her to the barn. She tried to speak but all she could mumble out is "Why?"

He carried her inside the barn and laid her on the slaughtering table. Tears began to stream speedily down her checks. The boy pulled out scissors and cut off the light blue stripped dress she had on starting from the bottom to the top. Pulling the dress off of her, she laid there naked crying unable to move. The boy looked her over and touching her body all over trying to figure out why his father said she was no good anymore. After a full inspection of her body he couldn't figure out why his father said such things. Her breasts didn't sag; her vagina wasn't ruined like the father had said. The only thing that had begun to age was her face. Her face had begun to wrinkle in the normal spots that all people wrinkle at, around the eyes and laugh and frown makes. Though there were bruise marks and permanent scares on her once perfect skin.

The boy knew what he had to do. It was what every other animal had gone through. She wasn't an animal though, she was a person, but that didn't matter. She wasn't any good to anybody or to the farm anymore. As he stood there looking over her again, he could feel the power inside of him growing and growing. The voices of the animal spirits speaking to him telling him that he needed her soul. The boy began to smirk with pleasure. He knew that this dissection was different but the principle was the same.

As Lucy laid there crying and able to move, paralyzed from the tranquilizer the boy began to get ready.

He knew that he had only so much time before his father would be home, but he didn't need to hurry too much. The tools laid out beside Lucy as she was finally able to let out a scream. The boy grabbed the needle and shot a little more into her so she wouldn't be able to make a sound or feel anything that was about to happen.

Laying the needle down, it was time to begin. He leaned over her and considered her eyes. This was the most fear that he had ever seen in any other animal before. This excited the boy, but he knew if he got too excited he would lose control and lose her soul. Placing his hand between her breasts to feel her heart, he felt the terror inside. The fear that she knew was that she was going to die and that the only thing she could do is pray. His hand moved over to her left breast and squeezed very hard, but Lucy couldn't feel it. With the other hand, he grabbed a make shift scalpel and started to cut down under the right breast. He repeated and repeated the cuts until he could cut off her breast. Tears and more tears kept coming from the eyes of Lucy. Mumble of prayer was coming from her lips. At the same time, the boy had cut off the other breast.

Standing there he looked down at Lucy who not only was afraid of death but anger in her eyes. Anger was a first for the boy as the boy only had seen fear to this point. This excited him even more. He could taste the death of Lucy coming, but again had to calm himself down. The knife moved from the sides of the chest to the middle by this point. He began to cut down the middle of her chest and digging to the rib cage. With four extra slices to her, two on the top and two on the bottom, to move the skin out of the way better to get to her insides. Laid beside Lucy's head was a small saw that was used to cut through the middle of the chest. Carefully the boy grabbed a make shift rib spreader that he had made and opened up the chest cavity of Lucy. There he watched her heart pound and pound. She stared daggers at the boy, but only excited him more. He reached in and started stroking the heart almost like it was a cat. Looking at Lucy he starred with a look of caring affection towards her and she still stared daggers at him. With the help of vice grips, the boy clamped off the top aortas of her heart. He stood there and looked at her in the eyes, the windows. The heart started to enlarge as it had no place the blood until finally the heart exploded throwing blood and heart pieces everywhere. With the last looks of no more anger just fear, the boy watched as she slipped away from life. Her eyes changed from color to the milky white that the boy had become very familiar with.

The boy stood over Lucy's body basking in his new collected soul. The power was stronger than ever before. The other souls that had been collected in him were to be pleased. The empowerment of nothing can stop you grew to its highest yet. Lucy didn't just give him a soul of fear but a soul filled with rage and hate. He felt the power thriving in his veins like it was about to burst out of him like Lucy's heart.

He wasn't done though. The boy grabbed the tools that he had created and began to dissect Lucy's body. He sawed the top of her head off and pulled out the brain. With his thumb and index finger he reached in each eye socket and pulled out each eye and placed them in a jar with alcohol in it. Next came off the arms and then the legs. With a clean swipe, the head came off easily for him. He started picking out the meaty parts of the body and the internal organs and placed it in the meat grinder, mixing it with pig meat to make sausage. Then grinded the rest up and feed it to the pigs.

Hours had pasted and the father wasn't home yet. The sun started to settle over the property. The boy sat on the bloody dissection table. Thinking like never, he realized that people may be the highest end of animals, but that was just it, they were animals. Death happens even to them and they can be made into food product just like anything else. Then there was the power that the boy had been feeling inside. It was different. It had been hours but the feeling was still there and he couldn't wait to do it

again.

CHAPTER 11

The boy walked down to the creak and lay by the side like so many times before. He thought back to the dream with his mother in it. He had wondered what it meant by having her watching him. Things were coming together now and the boy started understanding more and more. With the life of Lucy gone and her soul now inside the boy, he had become more powerful inside himself than ever before. Still things were still scattered in his mind. The boy didn't remember all the butchering that happened earlier. Things seemed fogy as if someone was helping or guiding him through the dissection. He found that with the right sedatives given by the boy he could do different things to the bodies and keep the person or animal awake.

More dissections of people had to happen. The boy felt rushed because he didn't know when his father would be home. He wanted to take his time with Lucy and go over the entire body on the outside and the inside. He

94

didn't want to just focus on the chest cavity. Every inch of all the animals at the farm had already been gone over; he needed another person to dissect.

As the boy laid there by the creek he listened to the sounds of the water trickle through the rocks and the whistle of the air going through the leaves of the tree. The birds had been chirping and the crickets rubbing their legs together to make the sound of crickets. All seemed calm. It was like the boy was in control of everything around him when everything stopped. The fast flow of the creek seemed to halt and the birds and crickets stopped singing. The wind stopped and seemed to pull the air out of the area and including the lungs of the boy. The boy's triumphant emotions had changed from proud to fear, the boy was frozen and could not move. It was like Lucy lying on the table not able to move. The silence made every hair on the boy stand and few tears went down his checks. Then everything broke as the sound of his father's truck rolled into the farm and parked. For the first time, ever the boy was glad to have his father home.

The boy ran up to help his father bring the supplies he brought back from town.
When he arrived, he found his father there with a woman, yet another whore that his father had bought home.

"Is that bitch gone? This is Megan, she's the new Lucy, but you don't get to touch this one! You ruined the last one with that seed of yours!"

"He's cute, you sure I can't play with him? What's your name boy?"

"He's a fucking mute leave him be! You know your place! Get in the house, and you unload all this shit, I need to take a load of meat up tomorrow, the butcher is running low. So, pack all that shit up and have it ready for me in the morning. Oh, and boy, you plant your seed in this one I'll do to you like we do with the animals and take your fucking nuts!"

The boy stood there dumb founded, planted the seed in Lucy? What did he mean? Was Lucy pregnant? Was the child his? He didn't see a child inside of her when he dissected her. The boy was even more confused. He knew how sex worked and why everyone did it, to reproduce. If Lucy was pregnant why did his father kick her out and not keep her here to breed like the rest of the animals?

The boy didn't have much time to figure things out tonight. He had to pack up the meat that he grinded up and pack it into coolers for the trip. With the truck empty, he would be able to pack it full. When he walked in to the barn, all he could think of was Lucy's naked body lying on the table. He imagined dissecting her all over again. As he pulled the coolers out and washed them he kept seeing the fear in her eyes and couldn't help but to keep thinking of them.

He walked over to the master freezer where all the grinded up meat had been packed. The most sold was anything pig from the farm and some beef. Lucy had made it in with the sausage links. Each container was placed inside the coolers separating each type of meat. The boy emptied the freezer and had used all the coolers by this point. Each one had enough dry ice in each one to keep the meat good until sunrise for his father to take it to town for the butcher.

After loading the truck full of the goods, he went inside the house. It was very late, a little after three in the morning and he had to be up in the morning to take care of the animals. Going through the door he seen his father passed out in his underwear laying half on the couch and half on the floor. Megan was naked lying half on top of his father and on the couch face down. The boy stood there

98

looking at Megan from the top of her blond-haired head, down her curved in back raising back up at the buttocks, coming down to very thin but long clean-shaven legs. After a few moments, the boy walked down to the bathroom to wash up.

The boy did a quick wash of his arms and face. He raised his head and looked at himself in the mirror, right in the eyes, the power was inside and these were the windows in which he could see it. He grasped the sides of the sink and pulled himself closer to the mirror to see inside to see the souls.

CLANK! Something fell and broke the boy's grasp of the soul search and the sink. He jumped as he had thought he was alone in the bathroom. He looked around and seen a hair brush from the back of the toilet had fallen off and fell in the tub. The boy had pushed himself up against the door from the unexpected sound. He walked to the tub and seen Lucy's metal hair brush in the tub lying there. Looking and staring at the brush, he tried to make reason of how it made it there but he couldn't. He left the brush and went into his bedroom and laid down for his two or three-hour night's sleep.

CHAPTER 12

The sounds of the truck engine starting woke the boy in the morning. It had only been a few hours and the boy was still very tired from all the events that had occurred the day before. The boy walked down to the kitchen to have a breakfast waiting for him by an overly cheery Megan.

"Hi! Oh, that's right you're some sort of mute. Why don't you talk? That's right you won't answer me anyway, oh well. I love to talk. So, does your dad. Not as much as me. I cooked you eggs and beacon. I figured that's what Lucy did for you guys along with other things. Your dads going to be gone a while, he's a little too old to keep up with me, I bet you could keep up with me just right. Am I right?"

The boy just sat there looking at Megan while he ate. He looked her over and he could see that he would like to take her up on the offer, but he had things to do.

Though, it was hard for him not to look at her braless belly

shirt with her nipples poking through the shirt, plus the

super short yellow shorts that had most of her behind

hanging out and the front was so tight it formed with her

vagina.

He stood up and walked straight out of the house

without finishing his breakfast. Megan stood there with an

evil little smirk on her face as he left. The boy went around

the farm doing all the morning chores and doing what he

could before his father came home. The meat supply was

low too so he would have to make more. Taking a few pigs

into the farm and quickly slaughtering them before his

father came home. There was no slow dissection or

collection of any souls today. Work had to be done and

that was that.

With the meat grinder started he could start filling

new containers and placing them in the freezer. The

freezer was only half full. The boy knew that was not enough but there was nothing he could do about it as his father had not bought any new piglets to help compensate for the thinning of the herd. With everything packed in the freezer he closed the door and there stood Megan with that evil smirk on her face.

"Hey there, what are you doing? Are you done?" Megan smiled innocently with a she devils look on her face. She wasn't here to learn anything about the farm or the barn. She kept walking toward the boy until his backside hit the slaughtering table.

"Well look a table right here. I wonder if I fit on it like a bed."

The boy watched as she sat up on the table lifted her shirt off and pulled off her shorts and laid down on the table. He looked down at her smiling, but the images of Lucy in fear began slipping in and out of his mind. The boy removed his pants and climbed on top of Megan but it wasn't her he was seeing. It was a cold, blue skinned dead Lucy he was seeing. He placed himself inside of Megan. In her world, she was having a very fun time with the boy, but in his world all he saw was a limp dead Lucy moving with his motions and none that were her own. The boy was getting close to coming to the end and Megan pulled him out right before so she wouldn't get kicked to the curb like Lucy had, but in the boy's world he finished in Lucy.

He laid there over top of Megan considering Lucy's cold dead milky eyes. Megan laid there catching her breathe with the evil grin on her face. She had accomplished the seduction that she had looked for in the boy. The fun was ending very quickly now as the sound of the truck was heard coming up the drive. Megan jumped down and put on her clothes.

"Maybe again sometime mute one. You're a much better fuck than your father." With that Megan ran up to greet his father. She had told him he was down at the creek sitting.

The boy gathered himself and cleaned off the table with the hose. Everything looked normal when his father walked in. His father walked straight to the freezer and opened it to see how much meat was left. He looked in and put down his head.

"Looks like we need more pig and more cows, next time I go to town I'll see what I can do. It's a good thing you have all that corn out there to start harvesting tonight. Megan, I need another late night without you. Bitch can fuck a hundred times better than that whore Lucy." As the father ended the sentence the farm door slammed shut. "What the fuck was that? Boy, you are fucking with me?"

The father and the boy both walked outside and seen no one around, let alone the fact there was no wind to push the door closed. There was no explanation to give for such an event. The father walked away and said it was the wind. The boy walked away also but to start up the tractor and to get the equipment ready to start picking corn.

The boy attached the equipment up and was off. The day had broken to the evening hours and then to dusk. There was a lot of land his father owned but it was handed down by the family like everything else on the farm. This was the first real year they had harvested corn in a long time. The last time was while the boy was just that a small boy, when the grandmother was still alive. This job was going to be a several days job and it was turning to night and he wanted to head back to the house.

As the boy started back to the farm in the tractor he noticed something moving in the corn. It wasn't an animal. It looked human. There wasn't any one around for miles and miles. Could it have been Megan? The boy stopped the tractor and jumped down to look around. He walked away from the tractor to go closer to where he thought he seen the person running. Standing there in the middle of the field and nothing moved, but whispers started from a distance. The boy started turning in circles trying to pin point a direction but couldn't. The voice had been hard to understand. There were sentences but nothing came through. The boy started to panic a little he started to scare even a little, like when he was a child and his father would take out anger on him by beating him. The air seemed to get sucked out of the area to the point everything stood still and time was frozen.

"Boy" whispered softly into his ear by a feminine voice. The boy ran and jumped onto the tractor and took off to the barn. The boy recognized the voice and who he feared it was, but it was impossible for it to be her, she was dead, and the dead stay dead.

CHAPTER 13

The boy finished all he had to do with the farm work that night in a panic. The thoughts ran a mile a minute in his head. Who was out there? What did they want? How did they move so fast? Nothing made sense to him. This was not under the laws of nature that the boy was used to. Things like this do not happen. There was no explanation for what happened.

After he was done the next step was to make it to his bedroom without his father yelling at him for being so early. Plus, the fact that Megan and his father were probably enjoying each other fully, well he was enjoying her. Megan didn't seem to want much to do with his father but did what she had to do to keep money, food, and a roof over her head. As he reached closer to the house he could hear them moaning, this was not going to be fun for the boy.

The boy slowly opened the door and peeked in to see where the two were at. He could see she was laid on top of the kitchen table naked with his father inside her having a good time. You could tell from the expression on Megan's face that she was not all that pleased with the situation, but was pretending to at least. The boy had no choice but to be seen. He walked in and kept his head low not to look at them, almost trying to make himself invisible.

"Boy! What the fuck are you doing in here so early? Can't you see were still fucking? Get out there and get that corn done!" The boy kept moving forward to his room. "Did I fuckin' stutter?"

"Jim maybe he's had a long day, keep pumping me baby."

The father looked down at her and grabbed her left nipple and twisted hard on it turning it purple bruising the breast. Then he leaned close with teeth clenched he said to her "SHUT THE FUCK UP WHORE!" Megan began crying.

The boy tried to walk away again but didn't get far again.

"SEE WHAT YOU DID! YOU made her TIT turn purple! LOOK! What are you doing becoming a fag again? You rather see my DICK? Get the fuck to your room queer."

The boy hurried to his room. In the room, he could hear his father continue to slap and hurt Megan, but there wasn't anything he believed he could do. He could hear Megan continuing to cry and cry. The boy just laid there in his bed in the dark.

Once things became quite out in the other half of the house the boy could finally try and sleep. The thoughts of tonight's events had pushed hard on his mind. From the corn field to Megan, he feared the corn field and felt bad for Megan. Neither thing made sense. Nothing in this place ever made sense. The only thing that seemed normal was death and that's what made the boy happy. He wanted to dissect people not harvest corn. Even still there was no one here he could dissect. Lucy was a perfect person. She had no family other than the family on the farm and his father threw her out.

The boy lay in his bed reliving the dissection in his head. He remembered having he naked body lying there paralyzed with only her eyes being able to move. The first cut, the second cut, thinking these things turned on the boy. He started to get an erection from the images of what he could remember, and new things that were coming back to him. He reached down and started stroking himself closing his eyes and running the images over in his head. They were not of the first night when she startled him or the many times she performed oral on him. Not even the three-way dance he did in the bathroom with her and the other woman. It was the tear filled and terrified images of her dying on the table. The masterful dissection of her excited him to climax. The explosion was one of the best he had ever had. As he was coming down off the high he opened his eyes and a blurry image was in his room, a figure, standing over him.

The boy jumped up from fear and was ready to be yelled at by his father or who knows what else. He stood on top of his bed against the wall naked looking at the darkened image. The image was unrecognizable and it didn't seem like a real person. He just stood there scared, naked and sticky. The boy heard foot steps across the room and looked and there was another figure standing there. They both seemed female in nature but they were blacker than black. He kept shaking looking at one to the other to the other. The boy looked at the one beside the bed then back to the one in the back of the room and that figure was gone. He quickly looked at the figure beside the bed and it

112

was gone too. The boy so shocked from fear simply passed out falling forward on his bed.

When the day broke the boy jumped up back to his standing spot from the night before. There was no one in the room. He quickly ran into the bathroom and showered himself off from the night before. While in the shower he lowered himself to the bottom of the tub and sat there with his eyes filling with tears and water running down over him. There was no explanation for any of this. Nothing made sense to him. There was two women in his room last night and then they vanished, they just vanished. This was not how the boy wanted to feel. He made himself excited. The boy couldn't wait for his next dissection and the power of the event to full fill his need. The need of uncontrollable power over someone like the rest of the other animals on the farm, but to do it to one of his own made it the best accomplishment possible.

That though is not what was happening. He felt like a child all over again, hiding in corners from his father. To hide in the fields away from the beatings, to making friends with the livestock and to never ever to say a word even until this day, a word was never spoken.

The boy dressed himself and brushed off what happened last night like he would have done with the beatings. He walked down and walked straight out of the house. Megan and his father were still sleeping. The tractor was where he parked it. He wanted to get out there as soon as possible to get the harvesting done as fast as possible so he didn't have to deal with it during the dusk or night times. He just wanted a peaceful day to regain his composure and his power Lucy.

CHAPTER 14

Out in the field ridding the tractor the boy rode up and down doing what needed to be done. He remained this way all day with the thoughts of what happened the night before being pushed to the back of his mind with all the rest of the bad memories that was held there. The boy didn't push being out long either. He pulled in early like he intended and noticed an odd vehicle outside of the house. The vehicle had words on it saying Police on it with the letters of 911 on them. He had seen the car before while in town with his father during the few times he could go. The man that drove the car was older in his late fifties close to sixty. The man was always dressed up nice but always carried weapons with him, but seemed nice. To the boy none of this made sense to the boy as he was a nice man, but carried weapons for a reason that was still unknown to the boy.

The boy parked the tractor and finished what needed to be done before over hearing an end of a conversation that was going on. The voices in fact were getting closer to him; it was his fathers and the police man coming closer to the barn.

"That your boy there? He's grown a ton since the last time I'd seen him in town. You think he knows what happened to Lucy?"

"The boy's a fucking mute, never says a God damn word. Probably fucked her before she left though, he was soft on her."

"Well then a quick look in the barn and then I'm gone." The police man walked around the barn area looked around at everything and then his father and the man walked up to the odd-looking car. "Oh, one last thing Jim, George the Butcher asked for more meat as soon as you can, the other meat flew out of the store. I had some of it,

116

some of your finest, not sure what was different but the town needs more."

"Ok Sherriff, I'll get the boy on it." As the Sherriff drove off he called to the boy to come up to the house. The boy did as he was told. "You heard him, more meat. I'll go to town to see about more cattle and whatever else I can get, probably more fucking pig. Also make sure Megan leaves, the bitch is too much."

The father went to his truck and attached the trailer and left. Megan walked out on the porch beat up and bruised. The boy looked at her as a tear came down her cheek. The boy walked up to her as to comfort her but that's not what happened at all. He raised his arm around her and grabbed the back of her hair and pulled and dragged her down the steps. Megan screamed and kicked as she bounced off the porch steps. The boy dragged her down the stone road to the barn cutting her legs all up and hands. She kept punching and scratching at the boy as hard

117

as she could. She even broke a nail in the boy's leg and it didn't even faze him. When they reached the barn, he picked her up bouncing her off the door frame and odd and ends until he arrived at his table.

He threw her onto the table almost knocking her out when she hit. She slowly started to move off the table when the boy grabbed her arm and injected her with his cocktail of drugs making her almost immediately going limp. The boy placed Megan's body on the table. Her eyes were tear filled and shaky looking around not knowing what was going to happen next. The boy had his tools laid out and sharpened. He was also able to find new tools that he wanted to try. First though he needed to remove her clothes.

Turning around and looking at her all messed up from the dragging knowing that he had complete control over her, he looked right in her eyes. He got close to her face looking her right in the eyes wanting her soul to feel his. As he stared in her eyes he saw a reflection of someone else in the room, Lucy. He looked up but there was no one there. The boy grabbed her shirt and yanked on it until it ripped off her out of anger. He cut off her shorts and panties. She lied there naked. Her body was bruised, his father did more than make her left breast turn purple he had punched her a few times in the stomach leaving bruises. The boy reached out and ran his hands over the bruises that of his father left. He rubbed her side feeling if there was a different in the skin and then caressed her left breast. Almost to say sorry for what you have been through, all will be over soon.

The boy felt a small pain in his leg and pulled out the broken finger nail that Megan had left in his leg. The looked at it then at Megan's hands, there was long finger nails on all of them. All nicely trimmed and painted. The boy turned around grabbed a pair of pliers and a set of needles nosed tipped pliers. He set them down next to Megan's right hand. Fear flew out of the eyes with tears,

119

but there was nothing she could do. He picked up her right hand ran the finger nails along his hand and then lifting it to his face and running along his cheek. He then slammed her hand down on the table and refocused. With his left hand, he grabbed the pair of regular pliers and placed her index finger in them for grip. With his right hand, he grabbed the needle nosed pliers and attached it to the index fingers finger nail. With a low and wiggling motion, he began to pull at the fingernail. You could see the separation at the end of the nail away from the skin as blood began to come out. With a few more up and down wiggles he could separate the nail from the finger with blood pumping out of the finger.

Megan lied there in fear but could not feel anything. He looked in her eyes again to suck in that fear some more. With no emotion, he quickly turned and switched fingers. This time he went for the middle finger this time there was some struggle to remove the nail from her the finger, in fact breaking part of it off instead of

extracting all of it. The boy wasn't to give up on his goal.
With a flat head screw driver, he could dig underneath the
broken pieces and lift it and pull it all out of her finger.
With an inner grin that he hid from her sight, he removed
each finger nail from each finger on that hand. There was a
sense of accomplishment that he was building. With Lucy,
he couldn't take his time, but with Megan he had a nice
long time.

With the finger nails a success he went down to her
feet that had dirt and scratches from being dragged to the
barn. These nails were smaller and took less time and
effort to remove from her with even less blood. This
pleased the boy very much. He didn't want her losing to
much blood and passing out or dying on him before he
could collect her power, her soul.

The only extremity that had nails on it was the left
hand but he had other plans for that one. He walked over
to his work bench and tin snips from the table and walked

around the table to get to her left hand. With the tin snips, he placed her left index finger in between the knuckles and squeezed. The bone cracked and crunched and was starting to cut the skin but it didn't want to seem to give so the boy grabbed the end of the finger and pulled it off. The cracked and splintered finger stuck out of the hand but there was more blood than the boy had expected. The boy quickly wrapped a tourniquet above her wrist to cut off the bleeding, and then he considered Megan's eyes she was still there barely. He wanted her to stay alive longer, there as much more he wanted to try. The boy shocks her head back and forth banged tools beside her ear to make her more alert. She started to come around but her skin had turned pale and her lips had become the blue color that always meant death was coming soon for her.

The boy walked to his work bench full of tools. He knew one experience worked but the other one did not. He had to be more careful. Looking at what was laid in front of him he grabbed a small razor blade. With a light cutting he started around her left nipple that was bruised. Not following the bruise but the actual form of the nipple the boy was able to but around and into the breast to the point where he was able to cut it off but didn't yet. With slow deliberate actions, the boy almost acted like an artist with the razor slicing lines from rib cage over her breast following the roundness. He looked at Megan in the tear-filled eyes the entire time. She stared back with fear and anger which pleased the boy. With a sense of empowerment, he began slowly cutting around the nipple and finally removing it from her breast. With the same artistic motions, as before he worked on the other breast he cut little lines into the curviness of her breast. The boy stepped back and watched the blood coming from the wounds, but it wasn't much as he didn't cut so deep.

This excited the boy to a whole different level. He could instill fear and keep someone alive while cutting into them. That wasn't just it though; this aroused the boy so much he was erect at the same time. He decided to take his pants and underwear off and climb on top of Megan with razor blade in hand. Blood was everywhere on her body he noticed as he looked over his current master piece. The boy reached down and rubbed her breast all over collecting blood and rubbed it on his penis in a masturbation form. With his bloody lubed penis, he placed himself inside her and started to thrust her. She looked at him in complete hate now. She wanted to kill the boy but she was still paralyzed and couldn't do anything. As he thrust himself repeatedly he started to cut her more. He cut her in her cleavage area up to her shoulders making a design of sorts. This kept getting him increasingly excited and he started to thrust too hard and started to cut deeper into her which made her lose more blood. He looked down at her and seen she was fading into the darkness of death. That's when he came face to face with her placed his forehead on hers and reached up and cut into her throat as hard as he could. As she slipped away, the eyes turning milky the boy experienced the most extreme arousal he had ever experienced. When she expired, he ejaculated inside of her. Another soul had been collected.

The boy pulled out of Megan and sat there bottomless on the cold table. He looked over his work, he was proud. He has grown stronger than ever before. She was covered in blood and so was he, but there was no care about that. All was silent in the barn, in the room, but there was movement. The boy saw someone in the corner of his left eye. He clinched the razor blade tight and looked and swung the razor in that direction. There was no one there. Then the same thing from the right of his eye standing beside Megan's body, he turned quickly again. There stood Lucy and Megan together naked looking at the boy with a blank stare. This startled the boy so much he fell to the ground stabbing him in the hand with the razor blade putting it almost the entire way through it. Half was sticking in one side and the other half out the other side. That didn't matter at this point, he jumped up right away to confront the spirits of the women but they were gone when he stood up. The boy ran all around the inside of the barn looking for them but they were not to be found. He knew he was in control of them not the other way. He had to get a grip on the situation. First thing first though was to grind up Megan's body and kill another pig to mix in with the meet. It was going to be a long night for the boy, but it was well worth it for him.

CHAPTER 15

The boy stood in front of the bathroom mirror staring at his eyes. The mirror was steamed up. He leaned forward placing his hands on the sink. The grasp was hard and painful. Tears fell from his eyes. He stood there wondering about what he had done tonight. Megan was hurt and had to be put down like any other animal out on the farm. Why was it then it didn't feel like it was something that needed to be done? What was it that he seen in the barn? It couldn't really be Lucy and Megan, their energy resided inside of the boy. It wasn't a free-flowing energy but one that gave him power. That's at least what he felt when he put down Lucy. Now though, he didn't feel this way. He was upset with himself and he didn't know why. He had her energy but it was different from Lucy's. Standing there in front of the mirror he could almost see the both in his eyes moving around. One in each eye staring back at him making him grind his teeth to the point his gums began to bleed and breathe heavily.

There was the energy he was looking for. There was the control he wanted.

The next morning, he heard his father return from the town and by the sounds of it he had bought some more hogs for some breeding. He didn't hear any women outside with him. This was odd because his father always brought a new one home every time he we to the town. The boy moved around and started getting ready for the day. As he put his clothes on he noticed that he couldn't find his knife that he kept with him. He shook it off and thought that he may have left it in the barn or in the bathroom.

After checking the bathroom for the lost knife that wasn't found he went outside to find his father smiling and unloading his cargo into pens. The boy looked around to see if he could find the new woman around to see what she looked like but there was no one. It was just his father and himself. This wasn't a good thing for the boy. He hadn't been alone with his father in a very long time. Lucy and Megan took most of the hits for the boy and he knew they were coming back to him sooner than later, no matter how happy his father was right now

"I don't know what you have been dong different to the meat but those fuckers in town love it! I spent all our extra whore money on more stock. You had better keep at it, because I can't go that long without my dick being sucked. Go get the meat you made up last night and I'll take into town. We need the money now."

For the first time, it seemed like his father was giving him respect. The father seemed proud or was money hungry and wanted more. Without a beat, the boy ran and did as his father had instructed and packed the truck up. The energy that the boy felt inside the night before was back as his father stood there watching him load the truck full of goods.

"I want the rest of the fields done by the time I get home tonight. I mean it boy, get this shit fucking done. I don't care how good the meat is you still need to do that shit too." With that he jumped in the truck and sped off into town.

The boy did as he was instructed. He went and started up the tractor and went out into the field to finish harvesting all the corn that was left out there. The boy still didn't like being out there since his experiences from before. He tried to keep his mind off things by thinking about the night before. The things he did to Megan excited him, it turned him on. He could feel her energy running through him. He thought about cutting her breast and lying on top of her as blood spewed out of all her cuts and then slicing her neck. To the boy it was better than what he had done to Lucy.

It had him so excited it had him erect out in the middle of nowhere. The boy stopped the tractor and looked around to see if anyone was around. There wasn't

of course. The boy was very paranoid out in the fields. He

jumped down off the tractor and stood facing the field. He

felt himself through his pants and started stroking himself.

Next, he unzipped his pants and pulled out his penis. He

closed his eyes and imagined Megan on her knees

performing oral on him as a corpse. The blood still slowly

flowed from her wounds, as she grasped his penis with one

hand without fingernails, bleeding all over his penis, and

the rest of his penis being sucked on by her blue lips. He

stood there stroking himself repeatedly. It was almost like

Megan had come back from the dead and was there

bleeding from her breasts and her neck. When the boy

came to full arousal he imagined ejaculating all over her

bloody breast intermixing blood and semen.

The boy stood in the middle of the field full of

electricity. He enjoyed himself. It was as if Megan was

there performing oral on him. That's how real it was for

the boy. He loved every second of it. The power of not just

putting down Megan but now images of ejaculating on her breasts mixing semen with the blood had him on a new high. Though alone out in the middle of the field, doing what he had done. There was something still eerie about it all. Almost like he was watched and the boy didn't like that. He jumped up on the tractor and started back to work from his break.

The boy did some circles around like normal but had to go clear to the end of the property. He normally didn't go back this far alone, his father normally did this part. The end of the property was a road that came out of the city and to the boy went to nowhere because he had never gone down that way before. He had only been to the town a few times and that was still a mystery to the boy. The way he was cutting the stocks of corn, the boy would go back and forth on this part of the property, not being near it too much, but seeing a car or a truck drive past once and awhile. After a while the boy started to slow down and look down the way that he hadn't ever gone before and became curious about what was down there. He wondered if there was another town at the end of that road, just like the other end. Were there people like Lucy and Megan down there also? Could there be another farm like this one that had a mother and a father that was nice to their children. Was it a farm that would end up just like the one he was on? A boy who hated his father and the father hated the boy? Could it just be the end of the world? Dropping from existence into blackness? There was only one way to find out but the boy had no courage to find out, instead he continued until he was done with dusk rolling in on him.

The boy headed back to the barn to unload what would become feed for the pigs and other animals. The fall harvest was over and the chill in the air proved he was done in time for this year. After packing everything away for the winter and getting everything settled for the night the boy stood outside in the darkness and lifted his arms slightly from his sides and opened his hands. He could feel the energy in the air and he was excepting it in. It made the boy feel powerful inside like there was electricity running through him. The boy stood there for some time until he heard the all too familiar sound of the truck coming up the drive. His father was home.

His father jumped out of the truck and walked straight into the house slamming the door behind him. It was clear that his father was not happy about something, more so than usual. There wasn't a woman with him; this was going to be a long night for sure.

CHAPTER 16

The boy walked up to the house and opened the door. His father had a bottle in his hand, no label, moon shine most likely. The night was going to be worse than the boy originally thought. He stood there leaning against the wall blocking the boy from the bathroom and his bedroom.

"Why you a fucking mute?" The father said with a heavily drunken slur. "I said…why…you…a mute? Damn it boy. I give you everything you need. Not some fucking thanks."

The father moved closer to the boy setting down the bottle on the kitchen table along the way. The boy tried to make a move around but he was grabbed by the arm by his father. He stared down the boy right in the eyes. He trembled inside hoping that his father would let him go, but this was not the case, a fist met the eyes of the boy.

The boy started to fall over but the father held him up. He repeated the punches to the right side his eye socket and temple. The eye was swelling along with blood coming out the side of the eye. The father let him fall to the ground knocking the wind out of the boy. He gasped for air out of his mouth but blood kept getting sucked in. The father lifted his boot and stomped the boy in his right hip, then his knee, and then a swift kick to his stomach. The kick to the stomach made the boy begin to vomit; he still hadn't regained all his air so now he was inhaling vomit and blood mixed with little air. The boy began to gag and choke on the vomit and blood mix as his father stood there above him laughing at him.

"Get up fag boy! Get up! Can't take a little beating? Wait until I really kick the shit out of you! Fucking queer." He gave his son one last stomp in the stomach and walked off to his bedroom where he would end up passing out.

The boy laid their barley able to move or even see out of his right eye. With his left arm, he was able to lift himself up a little to get out of his pool of blood and vomit. The boy was delirious and wasn't thinking straight. He couldn't stand yet and his insides were screaming at him to lie still, but he feared for his life. Not sure if his father had passed out he decided to reach out with his left arm and hand and start dragging himself to his room and what would be safety. He started pulling himself inch by inch not getting far fast. Having to stop and vomit or dry heave was not helping him either. The kitchen table was all the further he had gotten; this wasn't close enough to his room. He lifted himself up to the table and sat at one of the chairs. His leg and hip was feeling better and he knew after a little rest there he would be able to go to his room. More importantly he realized that there wasn't any of the women around to clean things so he was going to have to clean the mess up he had made on the floor.

He sat there for a bit. Blood began to dry on his face and around his mouth. His eye had swelled so bad that he couldn't see out of it. The boys mind was blank; no thoughts were entering the mind. He sat there with a blank stare at across from where he was sitting, which was just the cabinets in the kitchen. Nothing special, but he sat there sitting staring at the cabinets. Time passed as he sat there. The boy wasn't keeping track but he knew that he had to move and start cleaning but his body wasn't allowing it yet.

In the chair he sat, moving back and forth trying to get his body to get comfortable. Finally, he made it to a point where he could tolerate the pain. The boy was finally starting to come back to his own when he heard movement behind him. The floor creaked behind him like there was someone there. He knew it wasn't his father because his father would have made more noise than just a few little creaks. The boy was frozen and couldn't move out of fear and pain. Without looking he knew there was someone there leaning down closer and closer to the boy. He could feel breathing on the back of his neck and onto his ear. The boy began to panic he breathed in and out as fast as his beaten body would allow for. His eyes shifted back and forth as the breathing had moved from side to side without purpose other than to scare the boy.

"Kill him." A light feminine voice whispered in his ear and with a gush of chilled wind passing the boy with papers falling off the table, the tension vanished. The boy could feel an ease over him. There was no more breathing on the back of the neck and any creaking of invisible foot steps behind him. He pushed past his fears, fright and fought through the pain and began the cleanup.

As he stood there crippled over he couldn't help but to think about what had happened to him. "Kill him" the voice said. Kill his father? It was the only thing that made sense, but his father still had a use. There was no reason to kill him like the animals or the women. All the others had to be killed because of necessity or no longer a use of that animal anymore. Granted the boy did do all the work and his father did beat him, his father helped continue the cycle of life by going to town and getting supplies and animals for the butchering. To the boy it didn't make sense to kill his father yet, he still had purpose.

After the mess was done being cleaned, the boy limped his way back to the bathroom to clean himself up. He still had vomit and blood all over him. A quick wash to the face and to bed to begin healing was the plan. The boy turned on the water in the bathroom sink and made it hot and started scrubbing his face with a rag and soap. The boy's right eye was still swelled bad and took it easy over that area. He was able to clean the blood and vomit from his nose, mouth and neck. Splashing water on his face, to clean off all the soap, the boy had his eyes closed and reached for a towel. He carefully dried his face off and looked at the mirror to inspect the damage. With his one good eye, he seen the room had become very steamy, more than he believed it should. The boy started to get nervous. He looked at the mirror and he could see himself from the steam, but a cold chill was starting to enter the room. The light above the sink began to flicker to the point of where it shut off. The boy hit the switch up and down and nothing happened. The boy stood there frozen like he was in the kitchen again. Again, he could hear breathing beside him but not on him and a squeaking sound that would start and stop. The light began to flicker again. The boy started to feel a sense of ease again, just like in the kitchen minus the gush of cold air. Though the cold air that was there warmed up like nothing happened and the light came back on without a flicker. There it was, the words that was spoken earlier, Kill Him. The words had been written in the mirror through the mist of the steam from the hot water.

CHAPTER 17

In the morning, the boy awoke to his body being sore. The entire right side of his body screamed in pain. His eye was still swollen from the multiple punches. He could roll over to the side of his bed and get his feet on the floor. With his left hand, he slipped on his shoes and slowly stood up. He limped over to a pile of clothes on the floor and picked up a shirt out of it and put it on. The boy was so scared from last night that he only removed his shoes and shirt before he lay down. The next procedure would be limping to the kitchen and get breakfast before feeding the animals.

Upon arrival at the kitchen he found his father there sitting not moving, like he was waiting. The first thought that ran through the boy's mind was Kill Him. Still, to him it didn't make much sense. His father still had a purpose for living.

"Well fag, make me some breakfast. Get your gimp ass moving, I barley even touched you last night. Fuck your eye looks bad; you slip, fall and hit something?"

The boy limped himself to the refrigerator picked up some eggs and some bacon and began to cook for him and his father. Kill Him. The words ran through the boys mind every time his father cleared his throat or sat down his coffee cup. The boy even began to look at the knives that was there on the kitchen counter and thought how easy it would be to just grab one and walk over slice his throat and grind him up. It could be that easy. The boy thought though, would he want it to be that fast. Maybe, drugged up and awake, he had never dissected a man before. His father could be the first. Still as much as the boy fantasized with the idea of killing his father he still had purpose and that wasn't the way things worked in the boy's head. If you have a purpose and are not needed as food you lived. If you were no longer needed or food needed to be made then you were to die.

The boy limped himself a plate of food to his father and then sat in front of him. He then turned and limped to get his food and back to the table and sat down. There the boy sat there and stared at his father while he ate. The thoughts kept going on in his head and his father came soon to see that he noticed.

"What the fuck boy? Queer eat the shitty food you made. Need to go to town and sell off the rest corn you harvested the other day. Pick me up another whore so I can have a fucking meal. In fact, I'm done." The father looked up the boy and tossed the food off his plate and hit the boy in the face with the food. The father laughed as he stood up and walked out the door and left in the truck. The boy didn't move there was anger ragging in the boy for the first real time.

The boy never really had ever gotten made at anything. He thought everything that happened to him was just a part of life and was normal. The beatings, the picking at him, killing his animals that the boy wanted saved never once had the boy angered at his father at least not like this.

The boy stood up and let the food that had now lay on his lap and left it fall to the floor. He limped outside to the porch and stood there at the end and leaned up against the porch post holding up the roof trusses and looked out onto the farm. There he wondered a life without his father being there and just him running it. Getting in the truck and taking off into town doing the business that needed to be done. Butchering what he wanted and planting and harvesting what he would want each year. In his mind, it was a wonderful thought, but his father wasn't fit to die yet.

The winter season was on its way and the boy was to start getting things ready for the heavy snows. His father though had to slow him down with another beating. Things would be slow and would take twice as long now. His recovery would take longer too because of the work that needed to be done. That also assumed no more beatings would follow up to last night. Though the boy had hopes his father was going to bring someone back that would probably be here for the winter and would take the stress off the boy like Lucy did when she was alive.

The boy worked all day. He fixed fences, patched holes in the barns walls, and cleaned out stalls to bring cattle into the barn when a big snow came. He took cattle from one are of the property to another that was better for the winter months. The boy accomplished a lot of things in one day for being gimped up from his father. The night was starting to come in when the truck came up the drive. His father was home. The first thought in the boy's mind was Kill Him.

CHAPTER 18

The truck parked in front of the house like normal with his father getting out and a woman getting out. She looked different than Lucy and Megan. She had long dark black hair and her skin was slightly darker like a tan but not a tan. Her eyes blue was captive as they glared down at the boy. The boy limped his way up to the truck where the woman and his father waited for him to get there.

"Mute, this is Celia; she will be with us for a while. Get more meat ready I need to make a delivery tomorrow. The whole fucking town loves that shit you been making. Made me an ass load of money, you did." The father chuckled as he and Celia turned and went into the house.

The boy turned around and looked down at the barn and wish he didn't have to limp himself all the way back down there. The night had captured the sky and the night brought some winter chill in the air with it. The energies were strong this night as the full moon lite up the area for the boy to see. Everything seemed perfect as it reminded him of the energies already inside of him and the night gave him more to collect.

Once in the barn the boy took a hog and drugged it up so that it could live during the dissection and preparation. The boy began by cutting lightly into the side of the enormous belly and cutting lines after lines in the side. Every time he would get to an end of a line he would look at the hog right in the eye and see the panic that had set in. Granted the boy had only one eye to look at the hogs two he still looked intently as if he had both to glare at the swine.

The boy changed instruments and now could skin large parts of the animal's skin off the hog. This panicked the hog but it couldn't do anything about it. The boy had half a grin on his face as he jabbed the swine a few times

148

the stomach. The other half of the face was still swollen from the beating the night before. The boy became increasingly excited every time he stuck the knife into the hog. The energies began to flow stronger through the boy. He closed his eyes for a moment and to collect everything, to breathe in the smells and the energies that needed to be collected. When he opened his eyes, the hog was gone and he seen Megan lying there still alive naked and arms out reached for him to come closer. Behind her stood Lucy stroking her hair and her neck, moving her hands down to Megan's breast playing with the nipples. Megan reached up and pulled Lucy down and started kissing her upside down. Lucy moved one hand down to start playing with Megan's clit, which was followed by a moan from Megan. Lucy looked up at the boy who had become erect and was slowly walking closer to them.

When he became within arm's reach of Megan reached down and started stroking the boy through his pants. She moved faster and faster pushing and rubbing the zipper into the side of the boy's penis. He then unbuttoned his pants and let them fall to the ground. So, Megan began stroking him the full length and kept pulling his penis toward her. Lucy suckled on Megan's nipples while looking up at him. She then climbed up on top of Megan in turn she began to perform oral on Lucy which began more moans. This made the boy even harder and wanted to lose control but he kept his composure as Lucy panted and grabbed her own breasts and pulled on her own nipples.

Everything was perfect. The boy could see with both eyes and was no longer sore. He was watching as one hand stroked him and the other hand of Megan's was almost entirely inside of Lucy. Lucy was really getting into it. She was thrusting her body back and forth over the face of Megan and had her hands all over the vagina of Megan. The boy intently watched Lucy rubbing on Megan's clit and four fingers inside her.

Within a moment everything stopped. Lucy stopped pelvic thrusting and Megan stopped stroking the boy. He looked at Megan who looked back as she clamped hard on his penis and wouldn't let go. Lucy looked at the boy and started laughing as she pulled out the boys missing knife out of the vagina of Megan. She climbed down off the table still staring at the boy. She opened the knife up and Megan lifted her neck towards Lucy. Without letting eye contact go she put the knife to Megan's neck and sliced her ear to ear with blood spewing out everywhere and Megan still laughs. The boy tried to back away as the blood spewed out but she still had a hold of his now flaccid penis. He began to panic but couldn't move. Looking back at Lucy she still stood there naked with blood running down all over her, she still stared and laughed at the boy. With the knife in her hand placed it to her temple and jabbed it into the side of her head and fell over top the body of Megan.

In a flash, the bodies of the women turned into a dead hog on the table with his knife sticking in the head of the swine. His injuries returned to his body and his eye went back to being swelled shut. Blood soaked his body as he stood there naked in front of the table. The boy rushed out of the barn and ran down to the creek to wash himself off. He leaned over shivering as the winter night and clear sky had allowed for the temperatures to dip to where the boy could see his own breath. Sitting in the creek and splashing the blood from him, he could see from the moon light the blood wash downstream from him. The boy didn't hesitate in getting out when he felt clean enough. He hurries limped to the barn and put his clothes on. He was soaked but didn't care. What just happened to him over rode him drip drying into his clothes?

When he calmed himself some he turned and looked at the hog with its throat slit from ear to ear and then jabbed in the side of the head with his knife that he lost days before. The boy was confused and didn't

152

understand what had happened and didn't want to. He had

a pig to slaughter and thoughts were the last thing that he

had to do. Reaching down he pulled the knife out of the

hog's head and cleaned it on the side of his pants. The boy

just stood there for a few minutes in amazement, then

began to butcher the kill that he didn't get to capture the

soul of.

CHAPTER 19

The fall had come and gone. The winter had brought dustings this morning and some wind. The boy had finished the butchering the hog the night before and had it packed and ground up the way it always was. When the boy woke in the morning his father had already gone to town leaving Celia behind. The normal thing that his father would do, leave the woman behind. Leaving them behind is always how he got his turn from them. Lucy and Megan both threw themselves at the boy and he was anxious to see how Celia would treat the boy with his father gone.

The boy walked out to the living room where Celia sat drinking coffee and smoking a cigarette. They made eye contact as he went into the kitchen to get breakfast. Nothing had been left for the boy. This wasn't the normal, Lucy and Megan made food for the boy. Maybe his father hadn't given her the rules that the others were given about

154

living at their home. The boy gave a glancing glare to Celia as he started cooking himself some eggs. Celia just sat there drinking and smoking glancing up once and a while at the boy. She wasn't half naked either like the other woman always did parading themselves around the house.

"I'm not to talk to you or look at you. Your father was strict on the rules. He said you always fucked the whores that he would bring around behind his back. Why he came and got me he said. Said he wanted me all to himself. I'm not a whore like the rest of those bitches. Plus really, what would they see in a mute anyway, the fucking conversation?"

The boy ate his food up and walked out to the barns to feed the animals. It was clear that he wasn't going to get anywhere with Celia, at least not yet. After the first beating she gets she will come to see him. It's what the others did, and it's what she will end up doing. He knew that and was satisfied with that.

The breeze was cold as he walked around checking and feeding the animals. Once inside the main area where the boy had spent last night, he stood there and stared at the now clean table. The boy was raged with anger that he didn't get the soul. The rage fired him up on the inside. He could feel the others in there wanting more, more souls. There was none to have and there wasn't anything he could do until his father instructed for him to butcher another animal. Another animal could feed his urge of a soul but none of the animals were ready to butcher or put down. He couldn't simply just kill an animal for no reason. That would be wrong. He couldn't do it. It entered his mind as fast as it left.

The boy stood there staring at the table for a long time. His hands clenched into fists. He thought about each one, Lucy and Megan. The boy received his own sense of pleasure out of the dissection of them. He began to imagine each dissection Lucy first and then Megan. He analyzed each one to each little detail. The boy began making mental notes of he should do next time he was presented with the opportunity to dissect another person. As he stood there entranced into the fixation of the next dissection, whispers started to be heard behind him. He didn't turn; he recognized the voices as Lucy and Megan speaking to him.

"You should do something with her feet. You didn't notice how petite her feet were? Are you up there? You notice everything boy. You need to concentrate on the dissection of those animals more instead of cuming all over a pig while thinking of us." Chuckles of both Lucy and Megan were heard in the faint and distant voices.

"Did you like the time you were out in the corn field yanking on your dick thinking of cuming all over my bloody cut up tits? Maybe you should do that next time, cum all over her as she bleeds out. Oh, I know make her a new pussy right above her heart and stick your dick in there feeling the heart race through your dick. I like that one you will have to do that one, yes."

"I think he is ignoring us look at him all stone faced and serious. Are you mad at us for fucking your brains out last night? You didn't get you little piggy soul. We didn't need him with us anyway; there are enough male animals here for us to fuck."

"You should go get Celia and show her around. I think she would like the table. I really think she would love to meet us. We've both learned how to eat pussy out well. I think she would love for me to get my tongue up there and flick that clit. Come on, at least go up and fuck her so we can watch those big titties bounce all around. I bet she will cum real load too."

The boy walked up to the table and started to punch the table. Anger had ragged too high for him to handle. The voices started to push him even higher. Were the voices there and were they really that of Lucy and Megan? The boy turned around to see no one standing there. Neither woman was there. He was breathing fixed. The boy reached back and placed his hands on the table behind him. He began to slow his heart beat and the voices had stopped. He knew what they had said was true but he had to wait for someone or another animal to be butchered.

As he stood their hands placed on the table he felt soft female like hands reach and grab his wrists. The boy tried to move forward but couldn't move forward. He pulled and pulled but couldn't do it. One of the times he tried to move forward it felt like he hit someone in front of him. Like there was someone on their knees in front of him. He looked down but there was no one there. What he did see though was his pants unbutton by themselves and then the zipper fly be pulled down. His pants began to be tugged on until they slid down enough for his penis to fall out of his pants his boxers. There he was exposed and limp. The boy though began to feel a hand wrap around the shaft of his penis and then be lifted enough so that it felt like someone was licking under the head of the penis. With this the boy began to get aroused but there was nothing there and there was still something there holding him to the table. He felt a hand reach up under his shirt and scratch from his chest down to his penis which was now being sucked on by nothing he could see.

"I think he likes it. Do you like your dick getting sucked? You seem to like it. Consider it a thank you for bringing us together. The more you bring us the more we will make sure you enjoy us and we will train the new ones as well. Do you feel the warmth of her mouth covering your dick? Do you want her to stop? No, you don't want her to stop. You want to cum in her mouth. I know your close. Your dick always gets thicker when you're ready to explode." Laughter from women rang out

160

as the boy did just as the voice said and ejaculated, but there was no semen. There was nothing, not a drop. His penis was still warm like he was still inside a woman's mouth. He could see his penis making the motions and movements of ejaculation but there was no one there, not even his semen.

Laughter rang through the barn as his hands were released and the suction of his penis went away. The boy just stood there thinking. Did he just have a conversation with Lucy and Megan? He couldn't tell the whispers apart. He didn't know which one was which when he was getting sucked on and where did his semen go? Could the souls of one of the women have taken it? They did take his knife, but could they take that? Plus, what about more souls, he just couldn't kill to make them happy. Everything about the past few days made no sense and it didn't seem like he was about to get a break either for thoughts. The sounds of the truck broke the thoughts and the silence and he knew he better go see his father.

CHAPTER 20

"Where the fuck is that kid at? He fucked it all up this time!"

The boy tried to hurry to his father to see what he was in trouble for this time. He could see he was really upset with him. His father stood in front of the porch screaming at the top of his lungs while Celia stood on the porch arms crossed in fear with tears coming down her check. This was the first time for her but nothing new to the boy. The boy though did notice the anger lever was higher than normal and braced himself mentally for a beating.

"About fucking time! Where were you at? Down there playing with your asshole you faggot? Are you sticking dead animal parts up your fucking ass? The people don't like the meat anymore! What's so hard about making it the same?"

By this point the boy had come in arms reach with his father when he grabbed him by the back of the neck and gained control of his body and head. The father had pure hate in his eyes as he slammed his sons face off the front of the truck hood. The boy tried to fall straight back but he was held up by his father. Next, he gave a swift knee to his stomach knocking the air out of his body making him lean forward. That was what the father needed to happen so he could grab with one hand the back of his pants and the back of the boy's head and slammed it into the right head lamp of the truck breaking the glass and cutting the fore head of the boy.

"Stop! You will kill him!"

"Shut the fuck up whore or your fucking next!"

The father leaned over top of the boy and rolled him over to his left side. He lifted his right arm and left it lay limp over his head. The father kneeling at this point started to punch the boy in the ribs that were hurt before and that were never really healed. He repeated the punching up and down the side as the boy spit up blood with vomit and breathed in the loose dirt from the ground. The father continued until he heard cracks from the side of the rib cage. The boy never made a sound, but Celia ran to the boy's aid which turned the father's attention to her now.

He turned and struck her down to the ground. He crawled over to her and straddled her and back handed her back and forth, check to check. Until she stopped resisting and just started crying then he reached down and pulled her shirt off her and threw it. He grabbed her by the front of the bra and shook her up and down lifting and dropping her to the ground until the clasp gave way and the bra flew away too.

"I told you when you came out here to mind yourself and you would be fine and now look what you're

164

making me do. Hey fag is you watching? This is how you fuck these whores! You're going to do as your told, right?" Celia shook her head up and down to answer yes to him.

He reached into his pants and pulled out his penis and rubbed it along her mouth but she didn't open it until he slapped her again. Blood dribbled out the side of her mouth as he stuck his penis in her mouth and started force his penis down further and further down her throat until she started to gag and the projectile vomited upward spraying it all over herself and some on his father. With a closed handed fist punched her on the side of the head. This disoriented Celia even more too where she was slipping in and out of consciousness.

The boy just laid there without being able to move. Things were hazy for him from the hits to the head. Things spun and he couldn't control anything or even move. He laid there watching his father rip the pants and underwear of Celia. On the steps, it appeared as two other women sat and watched what was going on and cheering on what was going on. It appeared to the disoriented boy that it was Lucy and Megan and they were to get their wish soon of having Celia be with them.

"Hey mute you watching? This is how you treat a woman who doesn't listen and you got what a boy gets when he fucks up all the time. Damn, bitch that pussy isn't wet!" The father reached out his left hand and spit on it and rubbed it on his penis and then forced himself inside Celia. At this point she was worse off than the boy when it came to disorientation. She had no clue what was going on. The father crawled on top and started thrusting himself repeatedly. Celia's were glazed over and was barely conscious.

"Get up and stop him. You want him to have her soul? He doesn't know what he is doing? Yeah, we get to see her tits bounce like we wanted but that was to be while you had her on the table. You need to stop him before he kills her. Look at him he's still slapping her in the face. He is even slapping her in her tits, get up! We want her go get her!"

The boy pulled his right arm to his chest holding his cracked ribs and started to lift himself up with his left arm using the truck. He leaned there and watched his father flip over Celia and spit in his hand again, rubbed it on his penis and forced himself in her behind. Celia still didn't make a sound as the thrusting was cutting up her face and body from the gravel on the road. The boy pushed himself up leaning his left side up against the truck and started to move toward his father. The father paid no attention to his son as he lunged out with his left arm and tackled him off Celia and hitting his father's head off the banister of the porch steps. The boy crawled up off his father who was bleeding from his head, but not enough that any real damage could have been done. He was however knocked out and the boy needed to move quickly if he wanted Celia's soul for Lucy and Megan.

CHAPTER 21

The boy crawled to the steps and sat up the best he could. He had never struck his father but he needed to if he wanted Celia's soul to himself and for the women. The father lay on his back on the ground passed out. His head had a gash in it that has seeping blood out of it. The boy had no concern for his father's health. He knew what had to be done. Looking at Celia beaten and battered with her coughing up blood, she reached out for the boy, for him to save her.

"Help me…."

"Yes, help her to the barn and lay her on the table." Feminine giggling followed the comment. The boy looked around and found no one around but he knew that it was either Lucy or Megan. He knew that he didn't have much of a choice; he needed the power of her soul so he could heal. Plus, she would never be the same again; she had to be put down.

He reached out and grabbed her left hand with his left hand softly at first to gain her trust. She crawled herself to him and pulled herself up to his lap with his assistance. The boy looked down at her as she sobbed into his lap. He brushed her hair from her face and placed it gently behind her ear while caressing her check. The boy started to stand with her pushing against him helping herself up as well. They stood there crouched in an odd position for each other as they were both injured and needed each other to stand. Celia looked down at his father and with the ball of her foot she pulled her leg back the best she could and kicked him in the side of the head.

"Let's get in the truck and leave, we can just leave. When he wakes we can be gone, anywhere please let's just leave the fucker where he lays."

The boy pulled back and looked Celia in the eyes. He could see the tears, but through that he could see the pulse of her soul screaming out. It couldn't be that easy to leave. He would have left the farm already if it was that easy. There is nothing else out there but that one town, nothing more. He stepped forward toward the truck and she followed. With the wrist still clamped he grabbed tight and then started limping the both of them toward the barn. Celia screamed to be let go, she swung and hit him. She tried to claw at his back as she fell to the dirt road leading to the barn. Her naked body was scrapping and bruising as he solemnly dragged her screaming into the barn.

At the door, he opened it and he could see Lucy and Megan standing by the table. Celia was still at on the ground. He looked down at her and grabbed her around her neck and lifted her up some and dragged her in the rest of the way to the table. The boy then picked her up and slammed her onto the table with her screaming as she hit the table. The door to the barn blew shut and latched itself.

The boy looked up at Lucy and she just smiled at the boy. He then reached for the tranquilizers and stuck some in the side of Celia's neck. Within seconds her body went limp. The boy's body though was full of adrenaline and acted as if it didn't take a beating.

"What should we do to her? You didn't even get to fuck her, still can if you want sloppy seconds from daddy, though I don't think he came. Are you going to make her a new pussy like we suggested before? I bet that would feel great on your dick, imagine the warmth the heart brings"

The boy turned and grabbed a knife and walked down to Celia's feet. He grabbed the left one. They were both almost black from the dirty and bloody from the scrapes from the drag to the barn. He moved her foot around almost to study how the foot worked. Turning left to right, up and down, and then spinning it around in the circle while feeling her ankle and her Achilles heel. The boy placed his thumb and index finger in the lose skin between the weakness and the ankle and shock it back and forth. He gazed down at Celia who was crying and then at Lucy and Megan who stood by her head with stern looks on their faces as if they were waiting for him to start. So, he started. He put the knife to the loose part of the skin and shoved it through making a hole. Next, he grabbed the other and did the same. With these holes, he started by placing towing chain hooks in each hole and attaching each foot to a chain. He grabbed one chain and hung it from one rafter pulling her leg in one direction and then doing the same to the other foot pulling her other leg in the other direction.

"We like your work so far. What are you going to do fuck her while she is literally chained up? Kinky we like it. Go ahead and fuck her we won't get jealous, but we will watch." Lucy and Megan stood there without expression though their voices sounded different. They sounded excited and invigorated by watching the fate of someone else other than themselves.

172

The boy had other plans though. He wasn't going to fuck her, at least not yet. Ducking under one of Celia's blood dripping legs he walked down to her torso are and grabbed one arm. Like the foot he moved the hand around and around moving every finger and then feeling a little bellow the wrist. The soft part of the forearm that had no bone was his focus. Just like the foot a weak spot for his knife to cut a hole into. Not knowing better, the boy didn't realize that there were major blood vesicles in that area and blood poured out of forearm. He jammed cloth in the holes to slow the bleeding along with another towing hook in between it all. The boy then carefully grabbed the other forearm and cut a hole in between the veins the best he could. Again, he placed cloth in the holes with another towing hook. Like the legs he grabbed each arm and chained it to the rafters of the barn. Each arm was being pulled away from the body with the chains pulling on each limb tightly.

"Oh what are you going to do? I've heard of tied up before but this is a step that is beyond anything I ever been in. What's next? What are you going to do next? We can't wait and see." Lucy and Megan had moved to the other side of the table that was on the way to the door. They still stood there stone faced but with lively sounding voices and their mouths never opening.

The boy looked down to look at Celia in the eyes and there were tears of severe fear. The boy reached down and whipped them away and caressed her cheek. As he starred in the fear filled eyes he began caressing her breasts, each one soft, firm, and a little larger than he was used too. Her nipples hard from the cold and goose bumps all her torso. He slipped his hand down from the torso area to right below the sternum pushing and feeling and finding a soft spot. Looking at Lucy and Megan he walked down to the place he was pushing on and began to feel the very end of the rib cage. With his knife, he cut into Celia deep enough to cut the upper part of the fat of the body.

174

He only cut and loosened the middle up. Moving slow and calculated he was able to move the rib cage up a little making a hole into her body. He placed the knife down and placed two fingers in the whole he made and pulled them out and back in repeatedly. The boy created what he was suggested to create.

"Very nice, another pussy, one not tainted by your father's sloppy seconds. Hate that man. You though, you have created a master piece. Get your dick wet boy, she is waiting to come and join us, she doesn't have much time left she is bleeding bad. Let's oh yes that dick is a rock. Get it in her."

The Boy climbed on top of Celia naked and with his penis he stuck it in her as far as he could. Her eyes grew bigger and bigger. He could feel her heart race faster and faster. It was like his penis was inside her heart. The warmth was intense which excited the boy as he began to thrust into her.

"Oh mute, this gives a new meaning to titty fucking someone. Look at them big fucking titties bounce everywhere. I can't wait to play with her. Keep going boy, I think she may cum." He could see Lucy and Megan on each side of the table, one playing with one breast and the other playing with the other while their free hand holding her head still making her look right at the boy.

He kept going and going, thrusting like it was a real vagina, even though it wasn't. Time was ending for Celia her eyes started to turn the milky white, the point that he always waited for. This excited him so much he began to pull himself out and slam himself as hard as he could into her. Blood started spewing from her mouth and the chains rattled as the boy ejaculated immensely into her chest with her slipping away into the boy all at the same time. The boy collected another soul. Celia was with Lucy and Megan and none of them were around. They had disappeared, gone into nothingness, but he could feel them inside with adrenaline pumping. His penis was still inside of Celia as he starred down at her limp, cooling body. He

pulled out and climbed down and stood beside her and the

contraption he had made.

CHAPTER 22

The boy knew that he had to dissect Celia and
make meat for the town for his father so he wouldn't be as
mad, so he began the dissection. Instead of simply taking
out the hooks and unchaining her body he just cut her
limps off with a bone say. The boy took hours to dissect
Celia, longer than he had done with Lucy and Megan. He
wanted to learn more about the weaknesses about the body
that he had yet learned. Each part of flesh and meat was
tossed into the meat grinder. The insides, the intestines,
everything would be taken and placed into the grinder. He
removed her limbs from the chains skinned all the meat off
them until there was only bone left. He pushed the bones
to the side and grabbed him a hog and without trying to
collect the soul he tranquilized the animal and then put a
knife up in its jaw hitting the brain and killing it instantly.
The work was long and intense but was needed to be done.
Like Celia and the other women, he mixed the meat of the

hog with the body of Celia, cutting up large chunks of meat to match the amount of meat like all the other times.

When everything was packed up the boy walked all the meat up to the house making several trips and placing the meat on the table. It took the entire night but his father's wishes were complete. The adrenaline began to fade from the body of the boy, but he still could feel all three of them in his mind. Communicating, planning, having sex, who knew, the boy didn't, but he knew they were there inside. They weren't inside was his father. He was still laid outside in the cold knocked out.

The boy walked outside and looked down at his father. He seemed to have stopped bleeding but was still breathing. The boy leaned over his father and looked at him. Anger grew inside. The women were there looking through his eyes at his father. Urges started to form in the boy to harm and butcher him like Celia had just been done. The women that died in the boy's life had a purpose of dying. His father no matter how mean still had purpose and was not old, it wasn't the way things were done in life.

He reached down and grabbed his father by the feet and dragged him up the steps with his head bouncing off all three steps and slide across the porch floor. His father for the most part was still naked from raping Celia from earlier so the splinters that the father was going to have were going to be bad. The door was opened and the father was shoved inside by a foot of the boys shoving him into the house and rolled into the dining room slash kitchen where the meat was packaged. This way when he awoke he would go straight to town with the meat to make the towns people happy. It was made the way they wanted it.

The boy knew that this fight was not over yet either. He had never struck or even tackled his father. The boy would take precautions for the first time ever tonight. The boy walked into the bathroom first and showered all the blood off of him. The mix of his father's, Celia's, and his own blood flowed down the drain as he washed himself off. During the shower, he realized that the adrenaline from earlier was severally wearing off and was starting to take a tool on the boy. His ribs on his right side begun to hurt again along with his head which had deep cuts that needed glass pulled out of his forehead. He stumbled out of the bath tub to the mirror. It was all steamed up but three hearts had been made in the steam filled mirror. He knew it was from the women. He took a towel and whipped it clean and seen the deep lacerations in his forehead.

"You need sewed up. Sit on the toilet." He turned and there stood Celia with the same stone face that Lucy and Megan had earlier. The boy did as instructed and sat on the toilet and let her takes the needle and sewing string and sewed up the cuts on his forehead.

"There good as new. I am told I am to help take care of you. That's what the others say. They say we are to do things for you to make you feel better. Anything means anything to them. I know you just got off a little bit ago inside my chest and into my heart, but I think your young enough to get a little treat."

Celia lowered herself to her knees and moved the towel from his penis and placed it in her mouth. He wasn't erect yet but the longer her mouth held it in there and the way she twirled her tongue around his penis not taking long for him become erect. She moved her head back and forth faster and faster. When she could tell he was going to ejaculate she continued to pump but not suck his penis.

"Ever cum on a face? You like the power; this is the most over powering feeling you can have without killing someone. Stand up and spew it all over my face, come on I want it all over."

The boy did as instructed and stood above her stroking himself with her licking the tip of his dick to help get him to the point of where he did ejaculate all over the face of Celia. She grabbed his penis and sucked out the little bit that always gets left behind, and began rubbing her face all over with his penis pushing the ejaculation all over her face.

"See I told you, you would like it." As she sat there on her knees and in a blink vanishing right before his eyes she was gone. She was right though, he did like the power it gave him. It wasn't the same as the butchering but it was a good fix for him.

The boy moved quietly from the bathroom to the bedroom. Once inside he moved a dresser he had in front of the door so the father couldn't get in there in a few hours when he wakes. When he turned to jump into bed Lucy laid there under the covers, waiting for him to join. So, he did. He placed his back to her naked body, she held him tight as he fell asleep.

CHAPTER 23

The next morning the boy didn't hear anything. For the first time he slept in longer than sun rise. When he awoke Lucy was gone from the bed. He raised himself up as gingerly as possible and sat at the edge of the bed with his left hand holding his right side. His head throbbed from the hit off of the truck. He felt the stitches on his head that Celia had put on his forehead.

Things were getting out of control for the boy. He had reached a point last night that wouldn't fly with his father. His father was probably waiting for him on the other side of the door waiting to beat him. Never once had the boy ever stood up and struck his father. The boy always figured he would die if he fought back at all. Plus, he did catch his father off guard. Though he couldn't let his father have Celia, Lucy and Megan wanted her too bad for him to disappoint them. If it meant a soul, the boy would have to and will always fight for one for now on.

184

The boy stood up gingerly and walked over to the dresser and moved it out of the way of the door far enough to get out of his room. The boy walked down to the kitchen where he left his father and the packed meat for the town. Both were gone. His father must have taken the meat to town to sell to make up for the poor quality of before. So, without panic the boy sat down at the kitchen table and sat back and rested. He sat there and closed his eyes to listen to the silence, but the silence never lasts long.

"Scrambled or dippy...He likes them dippy, easier to make. He is easy to please. He hit Jim last night to save us. Reward is what is in store for you. We wouldn't count on daddy coming home anytime soon, his pride will be hurt too badly." Giggles rang through the kitchen.

The boy opened his eyes and there sat Celia and Megan. Without turning around to see her, he could hear Lucy moving around making the eggs. The women still showed no emotion as they sat there and stared at the boy. Their eyes were permanently milky white from their death and their skin pale with a blue tint mainly in the lips. They wore what they did the day they died and they didn't move. When he could hear them and their lips never even moved. Lucy floated over to the boy and laid the plate in front of him. Her feet touched the floor but they never moved. The only time it seemed like they moved normally was when they had sex. It confused and puzzled the boy.

"Go on and eat, not like we poisoned them or anything. When you're done we can all go play in the shower we think. Your reward for saving Celia, should be fucking all three of us in the shower at the same time."

The boy liked the sound of that. He stood up and so did the women and started moving to the bathroom when the sounds of a vehicle, not the truck, but a car up the drive. The boy swung his head around to look out the window, it was a police car. The police officer from before

186

asking about Lucy was back. In an instant the women vanished. The boy hobbled to the door and limped his way out the door. The police officer had already removed himself from the car and was standing at the steps.

"Hey boy, you look like you went to battle last night. I saw your father in town earlier and he looked a little rough too. I asked him how last night was up here at the farm and he said everything was fine, just fine. Now I know your father and he is one of the biggest drunks I ever knew and the biggest liar I know. Boy, I know you don't talk, you're like some sort of mute or something and you don't have to answer, but I am going to have a look around today."

The officer moved his way past the boy and into the house and looked around for a short while. He checked his father's room, the bathroom and the boy's room also. He walked back out to the living room where the boy stood leaning up against the wall. The officer walked toward the boy and lifted his shirt a little and could see the bruising from the beating.

"He does that to you? Looks like you can take one hell of a beating. Can't do anything for you anymore now that you're eighteen, you need to be the one to press the charges but you don't speak."

Eighteen? The boy had no clue that he was that old. He had lost track long ago what his age was or even his fathers. What charges was the officer speaking of? Did he owe something to someone? The boy grew more confused the more the officer talked. Plus, how did he know so much about the boy?

"I know there was a Celia Brink up here at the farm. Your father said he didn't see her this morning before he left. Odd how that's two women that have disappeared after being out at this farm, I don't think you did anything, but your father. I could see your father getting a little drunk and accidently giving a bad beating to Ms. Brink and killing her. Is that what happened last night? You try and step in and try to help out Celia? What about Lucy Moon? Is that what happened to her? Are they buried out here on the farm somewhere? Come on I know you know how to make words come out of that mouth. Help me help you."

The officer started towards the door and walked outside. It seemed to the boy that all was over for the officer and his questions were done and going to leave. He walked down the steps but kept walking down the road towards the barn. There was still drag marks on the ground from dragging Celia's body and it was obvious he was following that and the drips of blood on the ground. He kept walking and turning and looking at the boy to see where he was. The officer unbuttoned his gun and had his hand on it. When at the barn he still had a hand on the gun and then one on the door knob. He took one last look at the

189

boy as he stood there just watching the officer to open the

barn.

CHAPTER 24

As he turned the door knob he opened it slowly and quietly not to make a sound. He moved slowly into the barn looking down seeing blood from the scrapping and the dragging. He followed with his eyes the trail of blood and beaten path to a skeleton that hadn't been put through the bone grinder yet. On top of the skeletal system was the head of Celia. The officer turned wide and looked over his shoulder at the boy who remained motionless. In front of him stood all three women shaking their heads up and down telling the boy the officer needed to be put down.

The boy full of adrenaline that had been building the entire slow walk down to the barn burst outward toward the officer wrapping his arms around him while spearing his back into the table. The hit was hard enough almost snap the officer in half and shot pain through his body releasing his hold on the gun which left the opportunity for the boy to grab it from the holster and hold it against the officer. He pushed the officer to the table and laid there stunned and didn't move or say anything. The realization for the officer was that he knew now where the women had gone to now.

The boy circled the officer on the table with the gun pointed at him the whole time so he couldn't go anywhere. With his other hand, he picked up tranquilizers and moved to the officer's neck. The officer tried to fight away the gun but the boy injected him and made him limp and paralyzed but still awake like the others but twitchy. This was his first man and he is heavier than the petite women that were on the table before so he injected a little more into him to keep him still and awake.

The women walked up to the table and looked down at the officer. From the motions of his eyes you could tell he could see the women. He kept looking at the three and then back to the boy who had by this point grabbed a pair of scissors and started cutting off his

192

clothes starting at the bottom of his pants. The boy cut up

each pant leg and could remove the pants from the lower

half of the officer along with his special police belt. From

there he grabbed his shirt and just ripped off his shirt and

cut what needed to be cut to get it off the officer. The boy

then moved back to his feet and removed his boots and

socks. Lastly the boxers were cut exposing the officer's

penis. The officer was well in doweled and seemed to

excite the women without any emotion but the sounds they

were making made them very happy.

"Oh, look at that big boy. Damn that thing is nice

and think. I want to ride him until I cum all over the place.

We can't fuck him, who knows when we will get a penis

like this again? The boy is nice but not like this." The

women looked up at the boy and he slammed his fist

against the table in disapproval.

"What are you going to do to him? You never had

to put down a man? You aren't into men, are you? You

want to put him in your ass? I hear there are men that like
that."

The boy just glared at the women with anger. He
wanted to eliminate the problem that the women were
giving him. So, he grabbed a scalpel and grabbed the shaft
of his penis and took the knife to the underside of the limp
penis and cut it from the base to the top splitting it so it
opened but not into to two pieces. Next, he grabbed the
testacies and cut open the sack exposing the balls from the
sack. There they lay on the table. Two round ball things
and connected to tubing looking like veins but weren't.
The boy reached for the scissors and cut them off at the
base. The man was sobbing profusely. There was no calm
in his eyes. The women looked over what the boy was
doing as he grabbed the mutilated penis and shoved it
inside the officer. The boy gave the officer a sex change.
He walked up to the top of the officer after admiring his
work and looked at the officer right in the eyes and all they

were was sick and disgusted at the boy. He still had rage in him and wanted to fight. He wasn't going out easily.

The boy looked at the women. They stood there stone faced with no emotion. He could feel their energy passing through him. Every wrong thing a man did to them they wanted the boy to make the officer suffer a hundred times worse. He grabbed his scrapple and started to slide it over his body and cutting him with small little paper like cuts here and there on his body. The boy looked down at the officer's eyes again, he was beginning to fade. He was bleeding a lot from his new-found woman hood and it wasn't long now. The boy set down the knife and glared into the officer's eyes where tear filled but was still fighting it, trying to be a man about things. The boy wrapped both hands around his neck and began to choke him slowly harder and harder to where he couldn't breather. The less he could breathe the closer the boy's face came to the officers. He stared straight into the windows and there was his soul waiting to be taken. His eyes began to twitch and turn milky white. Finally, though the neck snapped and he was gone.

"Good job boy. We need to get rid of his car though and clean up second before Jim gets home or any other police show up looking for that one. Maybe in the equipment barn for the car, that's where it should be hidden. Go fast, we haven't much time."

The boy ran up to the car. His body was fully energized and felt different than with the women. He felt tougher and able to accomplish much more. It felt like his ribs had healed and that his muscles had become stronger. He jumped in the car and drove the best he could down the hill and into the equipment barn. Once the car has inside, old bales of hay covered the car with a tractor and other loose articles of tools covering the neatly placed pile of hiding ness.

As the boy walked out of the equipment barn the father showed up to the house. He stepped out of the truck and stood there and starred at the boy. The boy had no limp but the father did. He showed it when he climbed up the steps and walked into the house. The walked into the barn and began the butchering of the officer. He killed another pig also like the night before, without care of the soul. He left another one goes. The boy worked all evening to get the meat all ready and packaged the meat up in its nice neat coolers. The boy didn't make any mistakes this time. He turned on the bone crusher and crushed both skeletons into small dustings. This would also be packed to give soups more flavors. He placed the meat and everything else in the back of the truck, it had become a cold night and he hoped his father would take the double trip to town.

When he walked into the house there stood his father right inside the doorway and wasn't about to move out of the way either. The boy wasn't going to turn around and walk back out. He had a date with three women in the

shower that he wanted to get to. So, they both stood face to

face for the first time.

CHAPTER 25

"Where's the bitch at asshole! You're her fucking savior or some shit? Boy you done fucked up this time! You think you can put your hands on me and get away with it you dick! You got her hid? You are fucking her now like she is yours! I paid for her not you! Fuck You!" The father grabbed the boy by the shirt and slammed him up against the back of the door.

The normal beating wasn't coming; the boy knew his father wanted to put him down for good. It was time for him to fight back. The boy could see the women standing there behind his father, which surged energy throughout the boy. Adrenaline began to race through his body. The stone-faced boy that took the beating would be no more. He grabbed his father's shirt which shocked the father, which made him push harder against him. The boy could lift his father, cracked ribs and all and spin him around so the father was against the door.

With the positions turned the boy came forehead to forehead to the person who had taught him everything in life. The things that helped him survive for food, which punished him when there seemed no reason for correction, and showed him that women were here to reproduce even though none of them had. The boy knew that he hated his father and that he wanted to put him down, but that wasn't the way yet. His father's time hadn't come yet and he still had a purpose so he had to live.

The boy backed his soul-searching eyes away from his fathers. He could see the soul, it was dark with blackness. There was nothing good left in this man but he still served a purpose. To take the meat to the town, it was the only thing that he was good at anymore. The boy had been to the town but it had been years at this point. There was no way the boy could conduct business without his father. This didn't mean he was going to let things happen like they used to. No more cracked ribs, no more broken noses, no more black eyes, and no more limping.

The boy pulled back away from his father but still holding on to him. He pulled his father close to him and slammed him to the door. The house was old with little repair and the door that was barely even hanging on its hinges and wood that had become weak over time was about to get abused even more. The boy slammed his wide-eyed father against the door which made him madder. The boy pulled him forward again and slammed him against the door again harder. The fathers face grew angrier and angrier. The door handle area cracked as it gave resistance. The fathers grasp grew as tight as it possible could. The boy pulled back again and pulled his father close to him again to get another gaze into his eyes, another looks at that soul dark soul. With all the force in the boy he slammed his father into the door breaking it. Wood shards went everywhere and the side with the hinges even gave way all that was left was a door frame.

201

The boy and the father went through the frame and were still clenched to each other. With everything in him, the energies from the animals, from the women and the officer to the adrenaline that pumped through him he lifted his father up and about three inches off the ground and tossed him off the porch. The father landed on his back hitting the back of his head off the ground. The boy walked down the three steps and stood stoic over his father. The father looked up at the boy and glared at him with shock and anger. He began to turn over to his sides, to his knees and hands, to only get a very hard kick to the stomach sending him a few feet into the air and rolling across the ground in front of the truck.

The boy leaned over and picked up his father by the back of his neck and the back of his pants. For a moment, the boy could feel the stitched wound itch for revenge, but he walked him around the side of the truck to the back. Once there he lifted his father to look over the edge of the bed of the truck to see what laid there. More meat and that meant more money. The boy then dragged

the surprised man to cabin of the truck and opened the

door. He stood there and glared at his father. Almost like

he was telling him what to do telepathically, telling him to

leave and go to town again.

"What the fuck have you become fucker. I give

you everything and you think you can fucking man handle

me? Fuck you! All this meat you keep butchering is only

going to make me money and bring me fucking whores,

not you, no way, your mute shit!"

The father slammed the door, started up the truck

and spun out spinning the truck around, dusting the area,

and sending rocks all over and hitting the boy. The boy

stood in the same spot as his father left and let the rocks hit

him feeding off the pain of the shale hitting him. His father

did this the entire way down the drive way until he

couldn't be heard anymore. The dust began to settle in the

winter air and for the first time in days the boy could feel the chill from it. He unclenched his hands and allowed the energy that flowed in the air to be sucked into his hands. Eyes closed he raised his head and took in deep breathes repeatedly. This winter had brought change and untapped energy that the boy never felt before. It raced through him stronger than adrenaline. It made his blood pump faster and fast. The boy opened his eyes and the dust had settled and there stood the three women that he feed from. The ones that had turned into mysterious things happening around the farm, to things in his mind being taken over with sexual hallucinations, to finally seeing and hearing them all the time where ever he has on the farm. They had turned into his family. Even though they were spirits with empowering energy that he had to put down, they were his family, not his father.

CHAPTER 26

"Very good, yes very good, he will be gone for a while. It's time for you to shower. Long shower, all of us in the shower we will go. It's almost time for things to change. Oh yes change is in the air. You can feel it. We know you can feel it. It's in the energies within the air. They talk to you; they jump up and down your spine and crawl on your skin. The energies are here with you always."

"Time to go the shower is on and steaming the mirror. The others wait for you to join them. The have even started without you. Things will be pleasant for everyone except your father. Your father will never see what you see. The things you have learned are priceless. It doesn't matter how many women he brings they will always be yours now. You control everything now"

Laughter could be heard from all around as all three women floated past him and went into the house.

The boy turned confused. How could they start without him with them still having them in front of him, maybe he was more powerful than he thought. The boy walked up the steps and walked into the house as there was no door there anymore there was nothing to close. No one was around but he could hear laughter coming from the bathroom. He walked forward and opened the door to a steam filled room with three lively looking women. The women looked as they had been before they had died. They were without the blue tint to the skin or the milky white look in their eyes. Sitting on the edge of the tub they sat there talking and giggling like excited women about to have the time of their dead lives. They were happy and seemed very excited. They were playing with each other's breasts and were kissing each other. Megan waved the boy over to join them. The boy undressed until he was naked and walked over to them.

"First a shower for you," said Megan and just Megan, the voices were not combined in speech. They were their own entity without the joining of the others. Lucy and Celia both moved out of the way as he stepped into the shower. He stood their basking in the flow of the water. Letting the warmth run down over him and enjoying the hands beginning to touch him. Lucy stood behind him in the shower and started to scrub his hair as Celia and Megan both in front but on the sides started to scrub him down from the top of his body at the shoulders moving down to the abdominal muscles into his inner thigh. Their hands not just moving down but now they were both on their knees each scrubbing a leg at the same time, then each a foot. Lucy started scrubbing down his back and then to his buttock. Then she was on her knees helping with both legs and feet.

Lucy reached around the front with her hand sliding from the soap around his thigh to his testicles and started sliding her hands and fingers on them messaging them. The other two grinned and giggled as they seen that Lucy had started to play with the boy. Celia stood up and started to kiss and lick the boy's nipples which aroused the boy to the fullest. Celia and he had never been together while she was alive but she seemed eager to do as the others. She reached up and pulled down his head to hers and began to kiss him. The kisses were romantic in nature and even seemed loving until he could feel his penis go into Megan's mouth and the boy's kisses began turning into full passionate kisses. His and her mouth opened wider and wider with their tongues passing and rubbing each other. The boy grabbed Celia by the back of the hair and pulled her away far enough to gaze into her eyes and then pulled and pushed her to her knees so she and Megan could perform oral on the boy. He turned and put his back against the wall of the shower. With a hand full of hair from Lucy he pulled her up to eye level and began to kiss her the same as Celia. Lucy pushed the shower curtain out of the way and placed her one leg up on the one side of the tub facing toward the door. The boy reached down

208

twisting his body while the others continued to perform
oral on the boy and started to play with Lucy's vagina. Clit
with one hand and two of his fingers inside of her as she
moaned he jammed his fingers in harder and faster almost
lifting her off the ground. Celia stood up and started to
play with Lucy's breast, licking her nipple and pulling
hard on it. She even began to slap the one not closest to
her which made Lucy moan even harder.

Celia was really getting into playing with Lucy but
the boy never had her and he wanted her bad. He
positioned her so the she could continue to pleasure Lucy
but the boy would be able to put himself inside her. Megan
laid underneath for the boy to switch it up from being
inside Celia and then able to pull himself out and put his
penis into Megan's mouth. He thrust and thrust as hard as
he could with him reaching back and slapping her in the
behind repeatedly while stopping to put himself as deep as
possible down the throat of Megan.

Lucy moved Celia out of the way and wrapped herself around the boy kissing him. She put a foot on each of the tub sides and put him inside of her. The angle wasn't right until she leaned back into the waiting arms of Celia and Megan. Lucy held on to the back of the boy with her hands clasped together. The other women started to pamper Lucy and started to play with her clit and breasts as she thrust herself into him. She continued to go harder and harder. The moans from the women started to come together like when they would talk to the boy. The sounds echoed into the ears of the boy. He could feel Lucy start to come close to orgasm as the insides of her began to enclose on the boy's penis, which made the boy get closer too making his penis thicker and harder until they both exploded together. His eyes glared straight into hers and then they changed from color to milky white. In an instance, the women went from warm fully alive women to the energy spirits that he had come accustomed to and created.

He stood there fully aroused by himself. As the women were there, was as fast as they had vanished. The wind picked up outside and was shaking the house. He could hear the women at a distance but couldn't make anything out. The boy stepped out of the shower and dried himself off. He walked out into the hallway with the chill wind coming in from the outside. This was made easier without a door. The boy quickly moved to his bedroom and was dressed fast, which would turn out to be a good thing.

CHAPTER 27

The boy walked out of his bedroom to smell smoke. He moved quickly to the living room where a fire had been started in the living room and was spreading fast to the furniture. The boy turned quick to move to the kitchen so he could get water but there stood the women blocking off the kitchen. They stood fast and was obvious this was there doing.

"NO! NO! It is time to take what is his. This all needs to go before he gets back. He can't have anything anymore. It is time for his reign of terror to end. It's time!"

"Yes time, let it burn, all the way, all the way to the ground. You must leave and go, go to the barn and wait on him. Sharpen the tools, it's his time. He must go. Time for him to move on, old, and useless, same as us, you had us move on."

"The end of him, the evil one is near, near we say he must go away from this world. Move outward so we can feed on his energy we need him, we need that inside of us so we can have more. You must give us him so we can have more!"

Laughter rang out as the smoke started to take over the house. The boy stumbled out of the house and out onto the porch and then down to the front of the house. He stood there as the flames moved from one room to another clear down to his bedroom. The boy stood there with no emotion or sadness about the house going up into flames and he no longer cared what his father would think about the situation either. The women were right; there would be no purpose for him anymore. It was obvious now. The boy had taken over the farm. They had taken over a while ago but were just recently able to take on his father without fear.

His father must go. It was the end of the farm since the women were burning down the house. The father would have no place to stay or the boy. The end was near for them. The house started to give way and began to collapse in front of him. The roof gave way to the fire and then the chimney fell down on top of the rubble.

The boy turned away from the blaze and started to walk down the road to the barns. He was to get ready like the women had instructed and didn't want to disappoint. As he walked down he could see the women moving around the equipment building where the police car was hidden. He could see flickering lights but it wasn't from the cop car it was more flames. They danced in the windows that started to break from the heat with a ball of flame rolling out each one that broke. The women were hard at work taking away everything that belonged to the father and this brought some joy to him.

The doors opened for the boy as he walked into the slaughter house. He walked to the table and stood over top of it remembering everything he has done on that table. The gates to the animals waiting to be slaughtered were opened and left go. They ran out the door as fast as their little legs would take them. The gate doors swung back and forth as the barn began to shake from what had appeared to be wind but it was unclear at this point if it was the wind or the women.

The boy walked around to his tools that he had used before and started going through the ones he would want to use and not use. He separated precision with the big meat hackers, the ones that would go through bone if necessary. The boy grabbed the injections and set them up and filled them up to the appropriate level. He was unsure how much to use since his father was like the officer and didn't know how much he would need to give his father to slow down and rest comfortably. The boy moved back to the knives and began to sharpen them one by one slowly to make sure that everything would be just right.

"Be ready, ready we are, you must be too. Your father comes closer we can feel the evil energy that lurks around him and they arrive before he does. His stench is unbearable; we should have never taken care of him."

"Never should we have fucked him. Never sucked his dick or taken his seed inside of us. We should have run we should have hid with you. No more beatings though. Nothing will be done to us anymore."

'Revenge, we will have our revenge. The asshole arrives soon; we must make sure the farm is ready for him. He will be very pissed but he deserves to have nothing, nothing at all! It will all be gone. The fields are on fire now and the animals have run away from the evil that rests inside Jim. Jim must die. Jim must die. Jim must...."

The voices stopped and the sounds of the truck were at the top of the hill idling and then they began to move forward slowly to the barns. The only one left standing was the one that the boy stood in. The boy moved around the table with syringe in hand and waited for his father to come through the door.

The truck stopped and shut off at the barn. He could hear the door open and close. He could tell by the slapping of the truck that he was still using to brace himself. The boy gave a beating to the father and he was suffering over it.

"Are you in there you are fucking asshole! What did you do? You are fucking idiot! Everything is gone! I have nothing! I'm going to fucking kill you!" His father grabbed the door knobs and twisted on them and opened the doors as he leaned on them. The fathers face was enraged with anger. Blood vessels to his neck were sticking out and as split came out his mouth and snot out

217

his nostrils from the rage. He walked and didn't see anyone. He looked left and no one, then right, behind the door and was tackled by the boy. The boy straddled his father and stuck the needle in his neck to make him go numb and limp.

"What the fuck boy?" His father muttered before he lost his ability to speak, but he still could see. His eyes grew as he looked past his son and seen the three pale blue women with a blank milky white shade to their eyes.

CHAPTER 28

The father was lifted by the women and carried to the table. The table that had taken many lives and given food for the town would be used one more time. This time it would not be used for food, but for revenge from everyone that had to bow down to the hate filled man and his fists. Bowing down to his mind manipulations of the world and his views of it brought the deaths of many. Each woman that stood over him each had a story. The women that made it back to town survived with their fractured and broken life. These women were beaten, raped, and manipulated to believe that this was the entire world and there was nothing back at the town for them.

The boy who stood at the end of the table by his feet never knew what it was like to be outside the world his father created and controlled. The back-breaking slavery of a son and the beatings when his father was in a bad mood was unjustifiable. He controlled his son to every small aspect. Everything the boy had known of the world

his father had taught him or made him believe. The boy

never talked even because of the man on the table. He

feared the beatings that he would endure, the ones that

came from his earliest memories of a child. Many of his

bones had been broken and have since healed incorrectly,

and the pain he suffered has in human and not right for any

child to bear.

The man on the table looked at everyone around

him, Lucy above him, Celia to his left, Megan to his right,

and the boy at his feet. The boy didn't inject the entire

amount into his father. Just enough so that he couldn't

move, and the boy was prepared to monitor his father

through this experience so that he would stay awake and

feel things that no other person had ever felt before on this

table. Before there was sympathy given to those on this

table and mercy was spared as it was an act in which food

creation and curiosity met. This time though, this time was

different. The boy feed off the women and their rage for

revenge. The boy never felt this type of emotion but was thrilled to be having a new emotion. The boy began to grin a little, even something his father never seen. Too bad it was his death that was going to finally make the boy happy.

"Hello Jim, remember us? We are what are left after your son feed us to the town. The secret that he had was us! You are fucking asshole! You brought us out here to die! He had no clue what he was doing! We have been living inside of him; we know how his mind works and what he is capable of. We knew we had to push him, and we always will. We are the same now. There isn't anyone who can separate us and keep up us apart. You won't be joining us though, you will just suffer!" Cackles of laughter flooded the barn and the wind swirled around blowing things around. The women and their hair didn't move. The chill though went up the spin of the father as he began to tear up and start to cry. He breathed deep and heavy and started to panic. The laughter started again

blowing more air around.

     The boy moved down to his massive table of

instruments that he had become too familiar with. With his

hand he reached down and grazed his hands against each

tool that was there to be used, but like always the clothes

had to be removed. He picked up the cloth cutting scissors

and started cutting his shirt off from bottom to top. Then

cutting sleeve to sleeve, pulling out the shirt out from

underneath of him, leaving his top half bare. Moving

around Megan he walked down to his right foot and

removed his foot wear and socks then cut his pants clear to

the top. With one side done he looked up at the

emotionless face of Megan and looked her in the milky

eyes. She looked back at him tilted her head slightly and

leaned in and gave him a kiss in the cheek. The boy

walked down to the bottom again and this time the boy

removed the footwear off the left foot and socks. He

started cutting and ended at the top of the jeans and slid

them out from underneath his father. The boy looked up at the face of Celia and looked her in the milky blank eyes. She too tilted her head and leaned in and gave him a kiss on the other side of the cheek. All that remained was his underwear and the boy slides them off throwing them off to the side.

There laid the man that created and caused pain and suffering for an uncountable amount of people. He laid there bare naked with his shame shriveling up due to the cold. This made the women cackle again. As his father laid there naked and cold on the table, the boy started to lay out some tools on the table that may be used such as surgical knives, butcher knives, pliers, a hammer, a spoon, and some nails.

"Where should we begin, we know you want to dissect, but we want to torture him first. Oh yes, we must torture him some first then you can dissect him. We all get our revenge then. Yes? Turn him over for us."

223

The boy did as he was instructed. His father could still feel some even and tried to talk but the sounds were incoherent. The boy stood at the head of the table by his father as the women glided to his behind. He stood there and watched as the women were communicating with each other but it couldn't be heard by the boy. When they were done they broke apart with Lucy joining the boy at the top of the table, Megan moving around looking for something and Celia staying in the same place.

"You liked holding us down. You really liked raping us, didn't you? Well then you fuck, we will see if you like what's about to happen."

Megan came back to Celia with a round handled shovel made of wood. Celia took the shovel and turned it upside down. The father couldn't see but he knew whatever they were planning it wasn't good. With tears filling his eyes, Megan lifted the man up so his behind stuck up in the air spreading his behind to see the anus.

Celia lifted the shovel up and placed the handle end up to his anus. The father tried to yell and move but couldn't. The concoction that the boy had perfected over time was perfect for this occasion and he was about to feel something he never, ever wanted to feel.

Megan grabbed the shovel and Lucy joined them as all three held the shovel they began to feed it into his father's behind slowly. There was no lubrication so it was slow going at first until he started bleeding. They would pull back and force, pull back and force, pull back and force until the blood lubricated the handle. The father tried his best to scream in agony but it was no use, nothing could be heard. The women continued the process until about ten inches of shovel handle was inserted inside the man. Megan and Lucy continued the pumping of the handle into the man while Celia floated to the top of the table and looked her milky gaze into the man's eyes.

"How do you like getting fucked in the ass? You like rape so much you should be blowing loads and loads of cum all over the place. You fucked me like this up on that road until your son saved me your sick fuck." Celia looked up and stared down at the other two women and communicated without anyone else hearing. Lucy glided up and grabbed the hammer and walked back to the end of the shovel. Megan held the shovel still and Lucy started to hammer the shovel into the anus of the father adding an extra couple of inches. Each hammer hit made his father's eyes look like they were going to pop out of his head.

This gave the boy an idea. He looked up at the women letting them know it was the boys turn to take out revenge out of the boy. The boy grabbed his father and flipped him over the shovel and all still inserted inside of him. If the man could scream he would have. He was starting to regain more feeling and he felt the shovel rip through him on the inside. He moaned the loudest pain moan yet. The boy looked down and realized that the tranquilizer was wearing off a bit but it didn't worry him.

With the women, back into place as before the boy began his dissection process. He reached down and grabbed scissors, pliers, and a spoon and laid it on his chest. First thing was the boy wanted to take advantage of his father's mouth opened wide moaning. The boy reached down grabbed his jaw four fingers in his mouth and his thumb under the jaw. This gave the boy control over him as he reached for the pliers. Before picking which teeth to pull, he ran his own tongue against his own to see which ones his father had knocked out. Those would be the same ones pulled out of the father. The boy looked down at his father and looked him straight in the eye and grabbed his upper right k-9 tooth and pulled with the pliers. He moved back the pliers up and down and back and forth until most of the tooth came out. Some stayed behind from it breaking. Then the boy moved to the right of that one grabbed it and did the same thing. Blood started to pour heavily out of his mouth and down his throat starting to make him choke and almost drown in his own blood. The tipped his head and upper body over to dump the blood out then used his father's shirt to hold up against the gums to control the bleeding. The boy pulled the next two on the top crushing the last one, not even able to pull it out.

"Our turn again we have something special for his balls. They were so big, able to hit a woman and over power them, such big and great balls they are." The women moved to the groined area of the father. The boy lifted his father up a little so he might be able to see what the women were up to. They had nails and a hammer in hand. Lucy had the hammer, Megan had a nail and Celia had a testicle held up against the shovel staff. All the women paused and looked at the father as tears came down his face. Without looking away from the father's face they took the hammer and hit the nail puncturing it through the testicle and into the shaft of the shovel handle. The father tried to scream but all that came out was a muffled moan. With the next testicle, they switched hands and positions but the same thing was done, another nail driven through the testicle of the man and driven into the shaft of the shovel.

It was the boys turn again. The women moved back to their positions overlooking the man who was clearly in pain which brought joy to all of them. The boy looked down into his father's eyes and thought of all the black eyes that he had endured through his life and there were many of them. He could see fear screaming from his eyes like so many times that the boy's eyes filled with tears and fear but it didn't matter to the father the beatings always came no matter what. Fist after fist, it didn't matter the father never cared and now the boy didn't either.

The boy reached down and put one finger on his bottom eye lid and another on his upper eye lid. He spread them apart as far as he could. The redness around the eye was showing and that's the part the boy wanted. Reaching up and grabbing the spoon that seemed out of place before

now made no sense to the women. The boy tilted the

spoon at the angle with the eye and placed it the red part

the touched the body and started to force the spoon in the

eye socket. His eye began to bulge outward and with some

effort from the boy, was able to wiggle the spoon behind

the eye. He then took the spoon and ran it around the eye

loosening it from the socket until he was ready to pull it

out. The father had pure hate beaming from his eyes now,

but that changed when the boy started nudging at the

spoon using the socket as a pivot and popped out the eye

from its socket.

He left the eye dangle out of the socket and moved

to the other eye that the father was fighting to keep closed

at this point. The boy fought with his father until the boy

stuck him with more tranquilizers in the cheek area near

the eye. He injected just enough to help him, but not to kill

the pain. With the little help, he opened up the left eye and

looked into it. Hate and fear shot out to the boy which

angered him some. The boy was less gentle this time opening the eye lids open and did a quick scoop of the eye and popped it out like the right one.

Both eyes dangled there like balls on a rope. The boy grabbed one eye and squeezed and played with it like a ball even. He moved it around as if he was showing his father that everyone was still there watching and enjoying the show. The boy even tugged to see if he had any give to the eye, there was. The boy had dissected a person from top to bottom while keeping him alive. There was a sense of completion except for the fact that the eyes were still attached. They boy took the scissors to the right eye and cut it off. Blood and some odd fluid started to drain from it. Next, he walked up to Lucy, paused, and looked at her in the milky dead eyes and she leaned in and kissed him on the mouth. He continued his walk and stopped at the other side, his right eye. He reached down and just held it in his hand for a moment and began to squeeze the eye until it bulged and popped spewing eye juices everywhere.

Muffled moans cried from the mouth of the man laid out on the table with no eyes, a shovel shoved in his anus and his testicles nailed to the shaft of the shovel. The women and the boy were not done. The boy seemingly knew what was to happen for the rest of the time without any thought. The boy did what seemed natural and started punching the lower ribs of his father. He punched repeatedly like what had happened to him so many times before. Cracks and snaps rang out from the rib cage as the broke and broke even more. The boy picked up the hammer even and then started using it on the lower ribs shattering them and making them into mush.

The women gathered down around the groin area again. Lucy started to pull on his penis trying to stretch it out as far as she could get it to for the circumstances that surrounded them. The boy placed a long almost piercing needle down by the women. He then moved to the top and lifted his mostly passed out father up and rolled him up to a sitting position and took the shirt out if his mouth. Blood

232

and vomit spewed out of his mouth and went everywhere and on him. The boy grabbed him by the back of the neck and pushed him forward towards his groin. The women pulled out the shovel some so he could be sat up right. Lucy had his penis in hand and Celia had the piercing needle in hand. The boy pushed his father's head down so his penis would be in his mouth. He looked up at Celia to give the okay and that's when she took the needle and placed up against his check and pushed it through to where it the shaft of his penis. Lucy helped angle the needle and helped shove it through the shaft and into the other check and out the other end. Megan had vise grips and clamped them on each end of the needle to set it into place.

There was his father with no eyes. A shovel in his anus and his testicles nailed to the shaft of the shovel with him bent over with his own penis in his mouth pierced in there forever. The boy looked at his father and there was still rage inside that couldn't be expelled if it was ever going to be. He didn't feel sorry for him. It was his time, just like his father had taught him. There is no remorse for those who need to go. That's what his father taught and that's what he was getting, not out of respect though, but by brain washing. The father was still barely alive but there was no saving him even if he found remorse.

The boy looked up and the women were gone. The boy was left alone, but not entirely, he still could feel them inside moving the energies around and pushing his adrenaline to a new high. The boy felt the energies moving around him and felt his father expire as he passed on and went into the boy. More energy only meant he had to collect more. The boy was done with the barn like the rest of the farm and grabbed a can of gas and dumped it everywhere including over his own father and lit a match and caught his work station, the table, and his father all on fire. The boy turned and looked at the door and it opened on its own.

CHAPTER 29

The flames engulfed the barn and surrounded the barn. Fire burs fell from the ceiling and the smoke flooded everywhere but the path out of the barn. The boy walked outside and looked around and seen nothing but flames everywhere. The women had turned everything into a fire pit. The boy looked down at the creek where he always went to think and decided to wander down there and clean up.

As he walked down he saw a woman standing down by the creek in a light blue dress with red flowing hair that waved in the cool breeze. The fire from all over made her glow like nothing he had ever seen before. All the anxiety, adrenaline, and revenge that the boy had felt was fading and peace was coming over the boy.

"You don't remember me, do you? I'm your mother, remember? I told you I would come back to you

235

one day. You have done great things here on the farm. You learned many things here and finally slaughtering your father took longer than I expected. You know you can't stay here anymore. The world doesn't see things like we do. See all your souls you have collected?"

She pointed across the creek and there stood Lucy, Megan, Celia, and his father. All souls, his souls that he had collected, they all belonged to him. All of them devoted to serving the boy, even his father. The animals the boy seen standing there, with a look of departure, the animals were released. It was the human animals that gave him his power.

"We don't have much time left to talk but you must go from here with your small army and amass many and bring the souls back to me. You need more soul's son, you not powerful enough without more souls. You should be at your strongest since you just killed your father." Sirens began to ring from the roads at the end of the farm. Both mother and son looked at each other and they both new their conversation was not going to be complete.

"Listen to me son. The world is as evil and mean as your father. No matter how much fun it seems people are having they won't take kind to you. You're not like them. You're better than them and they will never love you." The sirens moved slowly closer and closer.

"You know how to survive in the woods. Your father did teach you some things useful. I have faith in you son. You remember I am always here and always watching."

The sirens reached the top of the hill where the house used to stand. The boy ran across the creek and into the woods and turned to watch the firemen and policemen enter the farm. His mother was right the world was bigger than he thought it was. He had never seen so many people before.

"We must go, you must be protected. There are old hunting camps in the woods we can hide for a time. We must go. We are not safe they will kill us all if they catch us. We must lay in wait to pounce and take their souls one by one. They will never find us out her in the wilderness. Come quick."

The boy took one last look and knew he had to listen to the now four voices talking to him. There was only one thing to do, go and hide from the world. It was a world he didn't understand. His father never taught him correctly. He didn't understand, maybe he never would, but he is a man now and he must learn. The boy is no longer, only a man stands alone in the forest moving on with his life.

The End

After Thoughts

After reading everything that you have read, certain things should come to mind. Reality is only as you see it. There are a lot of horrible things that happen every day like rape, torture, and mutilation. To think things like this don't exist in this world makes people naïve and sheltered. The things people must understand is that anything is possible and most bad things that anyone can think of have already happened to someone.

To some, they may think that adding such pornographic images in this book is wrong or out of place. I believe that it is wrong to think that when you watch a movie that the people pretending to have sex aren't acting like real life situations. Most people now have pornographic style of sex or some form of it. You never see in a movie an actress waiting for the man to get a condom, or wait while the actor gets something to clean you up with. Sex isn't clean. Sex is fun and should be explored in books and movies in a way that is real. That is why I added those things.

I live in a world of censorship that shouldn't be there. From radio to TV to work, it drives me insane. I believe in a world that everyone can be free with thought and zero anger. Too bad the only place that exists is in my head and with a few close friends. Believe beyond reality.

www.ingramcontent.com/pod-product-compliance
Lightning Source LLC
Chambersburg PA
CBHW081208170626
46811CB00010B/3225